THE FUTURE IS SHORT

THE FUTURE IS SHORT
Science Fiction in a Flash

Volume 4

Edited by
Carrol Fix

Rogue Star Press
USA

The Future Is Short, Volume 4
Copyright © 2017 by Jot Russell

CONTENTS

Introduction

Science fiction lives within the heart of dreamers. For within a dream, there are no bounds, the laws of physics need not apply, and the dimensions of space-time are limitless. While the rest of us are bound by the rules of society, the strain of a weekly paycheck, and the obligations of our routine lives, dreamers are to free to fly.

If you could unlock your mind from these self-perpetuating chains and experience the infinity, what would you dream? Would you vacation to an underground city on a distant world, search for the bones of an alien race to uncover the plague that had caused their demise, create a universal language to bridge the divide between us and the beyond, or ride a machine to travel through time and change the course of history? The only wrong answer is nothing at all.

Welcome to our dreams . . .

Jot Russell
Science Fiction Microstory Contest Creator
Science Fiction Microstory Contest Group Founder

Bridges

January 2016

Theme:
Bridges – actual or metaphorical
Elements:
Things Carried

Champion
"The Bridge to Nowhere"
S. M. Kraftchak

Bridge to Nowhere

S. M. Kraftchak

What would you do for the love of your life?

Alexander leaned forward on his knees to catch his breath. He had arrived at the Bridge to Nowhere. His headlamp revealed a narrow rock bridge that seemed to end mid-air, a thousand feet above the desert valley, but it wasn't the real end, he hoped. Alexander's hand went to the round warmth nestled in the backpack on his chest. He had promised Rajiera that he would return her egg, their egg, to her home world.

He knew Rajiera was different from the moment they met. That's what had made him fall in love with her. By the time he knew her true identity, his heart only saw a soul he loved and for whom he would do anything. He'd never forget, as long as he lived, and, hopefully, that would be longer than ten minutes, their last moments together on the night she transformed and laid her egg. It had been exhilarating to hold her as her skin turned a vibrant, smooth-scaled green and her human features elongated to reveal her true form. And then when she had laid their egg, there were no words, except profound joy.

That night had also been the beginning of a three-day-long nightmare that spanned several hundred miles of rugged terrain. They had been laying face to face, their slowly hardening egg between them, when lights stabbed through each window and an electronic voice called over a bullhorn, "This is Homeland Immigration Service. Send the alien female out and no one gets hurt."

She bolted from bed with a screeching hiss, drew the curtains, and returned with my backpack and a handful of towels. Gently she encased the egg in several layers and slid it in the backpack as she spoke. "You must take our egg back to my home world. She will never be safe here."

"No! I'll protect you," I had foolishly announced as I rolled out of bed, hastening into pants and a shirt.

Rajiera grabbed my upper arms with her claws. "I love you for that, but you don't stand a chance against them. I'll buy you the time you need to get away. Go to the basement and pull out the canning shelf. There's a passageway that runs out to Croger's barn. The egg will show you where to go when you get there. Just put your hands on it, like this," she guided my hands onto the nearly hard shell. "She'll show you the way to the bridge to nowhere."

"But—"

"Go now while there's still time," she said as she slipped my backpack straps onto my shoulders securing our egg to my chest.

Just then, a window shattered and a canister of teargas clattered to the floor.

The rest is a blur: choking on the gas; fear of being caught in the long dark earthen tunnel; looking back to see our house ablaze; miles of relentless pursuit. It would soon be over.

Five feet from the visual end of the Bridge to Nowhere, an electronic voice called over a bullhorn. "Alexander, stop. Just hand over the egg and your nightmare will be over."

Alexander turned his headlamp off and slowly raised one hand to shade his eyes from his pursuers' spotlights as he took two more, sideways step toward the end of the bridge.

"Stop! Don't go any further. You don't need to do this. It's dead. It died in the fire."

"No!" He shook his head and wailed to the stars. "You don't understand. I loved her, and I'll never let you have our . . . " His hands slid protectively around the backpack. His body seemed to melt like he would collapse to the ground, but suddenly he turned his back and sprang to the end of the bridge.

Alexander heard the crack of several gunshots behind him and felt a burning pain in his shoulder and his side as he felt his body fall into the darkness.

***

The sound of different pitched trilling purrs returned Alexander's awareness. Laying on a soft bed of moss, he opened his eyes to see a lush green tree shading him from a bright sun. "Rajiera?" His hands jumped to his chest, and then fell to his side after finding the egg still there.

Three faces like Rajiera's transformed face blocked his view of the tree. "She's gone?"

Alexander closed his eyes and wrapped his hand around the egg. "Not completely."

S. M. Kraftchak. Whether voyaging the universe, or journeying in a fantasy world of my own making, I'm passionate about discovering all kinds of characters and relentlessly tracing their heartfelt stories so I can relate them to you. I love sunrise on the beach, sunset in the mountains and portraying Elizabeth Tudor. I have one dog who thinks she's a footrest, another who catches a Frisbee, and a cat who rents me my desk for open-window-time. I have three awesome daughters, and a husband who is my best friend, my harshest critic, and my most fervent supporter. www.smkraftchak.com

Discarded Demons

Jack McDaniel

She's a badass on a mission, a mission of revenge.

The Walther PCE dangled nonchalantly from her gloved right hand. She focused her oculars over the rubble and fallen plasticrete, toward the end of the row of warehouses. Where is he, she asked herself.

Demons hide in the oddest of places. Folklore and legend has them under beds, just around corners, underground, or in the basement. The Bakkle of Solorn is said to hide in the low hanging clouds on a rainy day. Ha! If only that were true.

Her demons, it seemed, hid in the things she carried, and on backwater moons amongst deserted and ancient warehouses. No worries, demons can be hunted and things carried discarded.

Movement. Half a klick away she saw him running. She grinned at that, the thought that he could ever run fast enough to escape her. She holstered the gun and began the chase, her long leather jacket flapped behind her, strands of black hair fell on her face before the wind pushed them back.

Two blade missiles, a gift from Ship, hovered at her right shoulder, asking to be used. But this was personal, worth the effort. The blades could wait.

She slipped on debris as she jumped a fallen building sign, nearly fell face first into the rubble but maintained her balance, barely slowing, and continued on. Her prey cut up a short flight of stairs. She redoubled her efforts. Closed fast.

She crested the stairs and saw him at the foot of the bridge that crossed a small and shallow river, the only one on the moon. She focused, oculars down now, but still saw clearly his humped shoulders and his squat, powerful legs, his oversized feet. The Consortium traitor was almost a caricature.

For two months, she had tracked him across three systems to this dusty moon that was little more than a storage facility. Her mission was simple: retrieve the node implanted in his side before he could deliver it to the Telerin corporation that paid to have it stolen. Something about bio-nano circuitry that could run off the body's own chemical and electrical systems; a huge advance that would change the implant game forever. Whatever—get the traitor—that's all she knew or cared about. Officially.

Unofficially, he was the last remaining member of the mercenary party that had killed her sister on Solorn just over a year before. Cale, her sister, was collateral damage in a student protest gone bad. The man she hunted, the one running across the bridge, was guilty of murder in her eyes.

To the right of the bridge a small craft descended and hovered on the opposite shore of the river, corporate mercs sent to protect the investment. Illegal, of course, but proving their intent and their connection would be near impossible.

He was halfway across the bridge as she reached its foot.

"Fire," she told the blades, and with her oculars up she indicated the far side of the bridge for the first, then plotted the second. The missiles departed with a high-pitched whistle. They moved to her left, using the bridge as a shield in case the merc ship fired upon them, though that wasn't likely. The blade missiles were new and would be unexpected.

The first blade came up from underneath the bridge and exploded with such force that she felt the ground rumble under her feet. She smiled. Ship's tech was nice, something that powerful in the size of a pocket knife.

Plasticrete and steel rained down. The merc craft reversed backwards and up to avoid the worst of it, banged into a warehouse before adjusting itself. No matter, the second blade had used the explosion as camouflage. It had circled around and come in from on high. It impacted the rear engines of the merc ship, killing them, and throwing the ship out into the water. The river steamed with the crash of the super-heated surfaces. The ship listed and sank partway down its body and rested on the riverbed.

Her prey was thrown from the bridge into the water with the explosion, screaming out as he tumbled through the air. She ran, jumped, and braced for the impact with the water, certain she would also hit riverbed.

The water lessened the pounding of the rocks along the river bottom. She found him, barely conscious with blood coming out of a cut in his head, and dragged him to shore, then belted him in the jaw before he could regain lucidity. "That was for Cale," she said. He moaned and went limp.

She cut the object out of his side with her laser knife, pocketed it, checked the body for anything else hidden and found nothing. She pushed a small, timed grenade and a photo of her sister into the wound she had just opened, sealed the wound with the same knife, and walked away.

Clothes wet from river water, wet hair matted to her face, she dripped as she moved along the walkway. The merc craft was on fire, no sign of the occupants, yet. She moved quickly. She would take the back alleys to be safe, the Walther Particle Charge Emitter drawn and ready.

The expected explosion came from behind her, one less demon to worry about, a little less weight to carry. And one more mission nearly complete.

Jack McDaniel lives in Colorado with his daughter. Several of his science fiction short stories are in The Future Is Short, volumes 3 and 4. His writing has also been featured on the A Creative Mind fiction podcast. His first novel, Agents Of The Undertow, was released in May of 2017. His second novel in the Pan21 Series, Agents Of Hope, will be released in September 2017. You can learn more at his website: www.agentsoftheundertow.com.

Rock

Marianne G. Petrino

A bridge for memories connects.

Pink Coffins lined the walls. These Shells were too young to know. The box and its contents had roots centuries earlier. But the one awakened might know what the Archaeologists had unearthed and place an accurate date upon it. That Shell waited in the White Room.

Sylvia waved her hand; a door opened silently. The glass bridge extending from the platform before her led deeper into the Collection. How many heartbeats before she reached her destination, secured an answer, and passed her practical exam as a new Keeper?

The woman draped in white gripped the box firmly. Far below, lights flickered. Students darted across other bridges with missions equal to her own. It had been a productive summer up on the Wastes, thanks to the vigorous winds and shifting sands. More would be learned about the Demise.

Her prize was dull in appearance. It wasn't a necklace made of mollusks, nor a yellow wedge hat, nor a wooden homunculus with a quaking head. Clearly, those objects belonged to persons of renown.

Sylvia bowed before the White Door, reciting the words of opening. "I respect the one that now appears."

Inside, the Shell, also gowned in white, sat beside a white table upon a white chair. This one knew many years, for she had lived to reach 100.

"We need to know," Sylvia said, reciting the expected words. She gently placed her object on the table.

The woman laughed, a booming sound that belied

her wizened condition. "Quite the prize, my dear," she cackled. Her dark brown eyes narrowed in her black face. "But I won't tell."

"You must!" A Keeper had to be firm, Sylvia thought, recalling her training. The Shells were often rebellious. But why wouldn't they be.

The unwanted question had haunted her. These people had been snatched from Death and preserved just in time, mere days before the Demise, as a living record.

"I wish to be free," the Shell demanded, "to know the Outside, and not to be stuffed back into a Coffin, aware of the Darkness."

Praise the Shell. "Your sacrifice is valuable."

"Only when you find something."

Bargain with the Shell. "I will tell you something of us," Sylvia offered, "if you identify this."

"And how many centuries will that have to last me, White Girl!"

Give a token. "My name is Sylvia. What is your name?"

The Shell's eyes brightened. "You are the first to ask, but I know you don't care, so I won't tell you."

A bell chimed softly. Not much time. A Shell could not be long out of its Coffin.

Sylvia sat down. Awareness in the Darkness was the only way to preserve neural functioning. But she wondered how she would have endured such torture just for having lived at a crucial time period.

The Shell's full lips parted in recognition of her thought stream. "Damn me," she grumbled. She waggled a knobby finger. "That fool thing is just a novelty. A home for a rock you can pretend is a pet, because a living thing is just too much trouble to care for and must one day die." She declared, "A waste of a few good dollars and part of the silliness of the seventies."

Not at all silly, Sylvia thought. A valuable lesson. Something worthy of a gift in return. "Thank you."

"Miriam," the woman whispered, scratching her cropped white hair.

Another gift. Sylvia said, "I cannot give you the

freedom of the Outside, not can I end your life." She hesitated, knowing if she took the action she considered, she would fail her test, and be punished. She studied the lined face. No one of her time would ever deteriorate so, but no one of her time would have lived as fully as Miriam had lived.

"But observe." She chanted, and the space before her gained color. "Outside!" Images shaped and changed, and as they did, she explained them to Miriam, who became transfixed with their strangeness.

Sylvia quieted, and the colors faded away. She rose, realizing the heaviness of the burden she had just set down. She could not stop the torture of the Shells, at least, not right now, but she was no longer a participant in it. She prayed the return to the Darkness would be more bearable for Miriam.

"Such a gift, blessed child! I have so many questions!" Miriam exclaimed.

"Another day," Sylvia said, knowing that the day might never come.

Marianne G. Petrino (aka Marianne G. Petrino-Schaad) was born in the Bronx, NY in 1955, and that single fact has shaped her entire life. She has survived too many professions to count. She currently resides in Arlington, VA with her husband and her cat. Her three novels and a travel memoir can be found on Wattpad and she can be reached by email at ninetiger@aol.com. (http://www.wattpad.com/user/MGPetrino)

Separated Siblings

February 2016

Theme:
Siblings separated by a catastrophe meet ten years later, on the
opposite side of a conflict.
Elements:
One is wearing a uniform that doesn't belong to him/her/it.
Last Line should be:
"I wish it could have been different."

Champion
"The Apostate Revenant"
Andy Lake
Unavailable

Brother, Not Mine

S. M. Kraftchak

What is the cost of betrayal? Would you pay it for a better life?

Mary Kate brushed the white apron smooth over her black, maid's uniform and clutched her bag to her chest before she stepped into the uptown space-tram. She tapped her credit band to the fare scanner and then looked down the aisle. Her hearts were beating so loud, she was afraid someone near her would hear, but no one seemed to take a second notice. There was standing room only at the back, which usually meant bruises from falling when the tram conductor played his sick game of rapid acceleration and sudden stops to see how many of the Rizjan he could put on the floor. She was glad she didn't have to sit there today. She never wanted to sit back there again. She had a new skin. She could sit up front. She hoped she was smiling properly as she eased past several other human passengers and found an empty seat. She hesitated and then sat.

"This feels good," she thought to herself as she slid over to the porthole. She kept her face turned away out of habit but heard the hiss of the tram doors as they started to close.

"Hold the door! Hold the door!" an oddly familiar voice called and she looked up as a Rizjan male inserted himself between the closing doors.

"Janzer, don't do that again or I'll have your alien butt banned from the system," the tram conductor scolded.

Mary Kate shrank in her seat as she watched the alien's head sink closer to his shoulders and turn away from the conductor. He regarded the other passengers momentarily and then turned his face to the floor. Mary Kate's eyes widened when she recognized her brother.

The tram unexpectedly lurched forward causing a chorus of squeals from the back where the cramped alien Rizjan passengers were toppled like bowling pins. Mary Kate gasped, watching the Rizjan male suddenly spin and bounce down the aisle before landing on the floor in front of the seat next to hers. Several passengers in front of her congratulated the conductor while another guffawed and then started loudly relating how funny similar incidents had been.

"Haasa? Get up. You know you can't sit here," Mary Kate whispered with a surreptitious glance to make sure the other passengers weren't looking.

"MarKa? Is that you?" her brother whispered. "What are . . .?"

"Sshh, you'll ruin it for me. I finally got a new skin and took over her job and everything. It's a really good life, much easier than living as second class—"

"How could you betray us? We were a team in the alien equality protests when we were Janlings. I'm sorry you got caught instead of me. When I last sensed you, you were being dragged away to detention. I tried for five years to find you. When I couldn't find you and didn't hear from you, I thought you were dead."

"That was a long time ago. I realized some things would never change . . . so I had to change."

"HEY, YOU, Janzer," the tram conductor shouted looking up at the video screen that monitored everything on the tram behind him. "You can't sit up front. Get to the back. Don't worry, ma'am, I'll make him move where he belongs."

"I'm fine," Mary Kate called back to the conductor. "He's just trying to find something he dropped and get his feet under him."

"But how could you betray—" Haasa whispered as he pretended to look for something on the floor.

"I think you need to get yourself back where you belong," Mary Kate said sitting up very tall when she noticed several other humans looking at her.

"MarKa? Why?" Haasa scrunched his wide nasal protrusion, bared his teeth in a typical demonstration of Rizjan dismay.

She scrunched her human nose and rolled her upper lip against her gums, exposing her teeth, and then whispered, "You don't know what they do to us in detention. I couldn't stand the . . ."

"Don't make me come back there, Janzer. I'll zap your gray-green back-side all the way off this tram."

"Please, Haasa, just go. I miss you, but I have a better life now. I'll do what I can, for our people but . . ."

Haasa made a great display of struggling to his feet. "I wish things had been different."

S. M. Kraftchak. Whether voyaging the universe, or journeying in a fantasy world of my own making, I'm passionate about discovering all kinds of characters and relentlessly tracing their heartfelt stories so I can relate them to you. I love sunrise on the beach, sunset in the mountains and portraying Elizabeth Tudor. I have one dog who thinks she's a footrest, another who catches a Frisbee, and a cat who rents me my desk for open-window-time. I have three awesome daughters, and a husband who is my best friend, my harshest critic, and my most fervent supporter. www.smkraftchak.com

Standoff

Chris Nance

A soldier meets his brother as an enemy on the battlefield.

"So, what now?" I asked, staring down the barrel of my Colt plasma carbine in a stalemate. I didn't get a response and I supposed I shouldn't have been surprised. My adversary was a fucking robot, after all . . . a mindless drone tied into the Scolax Continuance. Blasted meat-machine caught me by surprise while my back was turned, so I was more than perplexed as to why it didn't just shoot. When I slowly pivoted to face it, drawing my own sidearm, I discovered the face of my brother staring back at me, still wearing the remnants of a tattered Alliance uniform it no longer had claim to. Those sonsofbitches.

The goddamn thing only stared at me, his piercing gaze never faltering, and paused in time like a statue with fiery white eyes. You'd swear he was a mannequin, lacking even the faintest of tremors or fasciculations that come from a pumping heart and calculating nervous system. Instead, embedded alien circuitry relayed fiber-optic information to every inch, making the host a slave to the machine.

"Are you still in there somewhere, Pete?" I wondered and the damn automaton flinched, if only just a little. "Is that why you didn't already shoot? They weren't able to reprogram every bit of you away, were they? There's still just enough . . . just enough of you in there to hesitate."

His eyes remained fixed but he had a tremble in his lips, as if he was grasping to say something but couldn't form the words. The Scolax had planted a demon in him, a devil of technology built of glowing circuitry, and he was obviously trying to fight it. I could sense the gritting of his teeth and the tension in his muscles as he strained against the software that told him to shoot, that told him to exterminate or integrate any human he came across. Still, he just stood there without words.

My brother was just one of millions, huge populations captured and converted into mindless, obedient drones. Their objective? Honestly, I couldn't give a shit whether they were trying to take over our planet, eradicate us, or just grow their own numbers. All I knew was that they were using our own people against us, their very souls overwritten and reprogrammed by an alien intelligence.

We both joined up at the same time. Pete and I were young and stupid with some sort of romanticism of a heroic war. We were assigned to the same unit with a mission to recapture old Phoenix. Anyways, we were cornered and he was dragged away in the firefight just before we were swarmed by the marines sent to rescue us. I still wake at night from the nightmare, his terror in my mind as they applied the patch off in the darkness, my human brother merging with alien tech. That image of Pete, fighting and screaming as he disappeared into a horde of drones is what's driven me to kill every last one of those bastards.

Pete's hand was shaking now, the alien pistol starting to quiver. He dropped the barrel momentarily and I peered closer. I could see the suffering, if not from the glowing alien bits, from the sadness in his brow and the single tear that soaked his quasi-metallic cheek. "You can fight this, Pete. Don't let them control you," I pleaded and knew in my heart it could never be true. In fact, it only made things worse. His barrel corrected and his aim became truer.

There's no mistaking who shot first. A charged round pierced his chest and he dropped instantly, pistol sliding away. As the life faded from his glowing eyes and tech, I rushed to him. I suppose that weariness from battle, from having lost too many friends to the Scolax, made me a hardened asshole, but I didn't have any more tears to shed as my brother faded away. After all, he'd died a long time ago, snatched from his own humanity. At least I'd freed him of the struggle, the torment written on his face. Even so, I wish it could have been different.

For the last decade, Chris Nance has been helping people improve their health, working through his busy chiropractic office in Arizona. But his real passions have always been more in art and writing. Specifically, he's a huge science fiction fan. So far, he has completed several sci-fi and fantasy manuscripts geared toward the middle grades, young adult, and adult markets and is in the process of securing an agent to represent those works. Chris is currently working on the artwork for two children's fantasy books he's authored. When he's not spending time with his wife and three kids, or running his office, he can generally be found writing or painting. Chris also enjoys exploring the mountains of Arizona and traveling.

Truth

March 2016

Theme:
Truth – particular, abstract, ambiguous, relative, absolute,
disputed, lack of . . . any way you please
Elements:
A non-Earth or very-different-Earth setting
Forbidden elements:
Tears. Guns. Miracles.

Champion
"Truth Or Dare"
D C Mills
Unavailable

Truth at the Cross-Trails

Paula Friedman

Never go with your bother *to the cross-trail!*

If you have a bother—sorry, a brother—you'll understand. Don't ever go with a bother to a cross-trails on Earth-P.

"Go down any path!" my little bother—brother—Bolly commanded, eyes bright shining, shouting in the purple-pink Earth-P atmosphere, same as he'd always yelled back on Earth-1. "Any! Any! Any! Go go!"

So I climbed on the green seat of my Purple-People-Popper™ scooter, and I scooted off, brother Bolly on his Killer™ to my right, and down the trail we rolled, maybe half the neighborhood kids running alongside us, down through T'hronga swamps and Callimo copses and sawedgrass glowfields high to every side, all pinky-gold beneath the sky.

"Go down to where a path meets another path coming in sharply either way—from left or right," said Bolly, like a grown-up, then, sounding like his usual silly self, "THEN say. Then SAY. And then you will see."

I twirled a finger at him, but he didn't answer, so "Away, away," I sang, and "Hey hey hey" sang Bolly, and lots of the kids piped along, even little Lilli Beth, though she was having trouble keeping up, with her squiggle-feet (being half-Martian). So we sang, happy and free, all the parents at home or at work, "settled in, solid colonists, joyful," as Daddy always said at the biweekly work-sings, with Mom in her Mom-seat and Bolly and me, faking smiles, right beside them. Everyone smiles at work-sings, smiles and eats ice cream, and "You are BORED!" Bolly whispered to me last time, and I said "No,

I'm not," and "Yes you are," he said, and "No, YOU're bored," I said, and "Anything you say," he whispered, "goes DOUBLE for you," and I said "No, for you," and he "For YOU, including that!" and I "No, YOU, including that," and he "No, YOU, including . . ."

But anyhow, here we were, and Lilli Beth hung onto my pedals as we slowed. The pinky-purple air smelled green; flowers gleamed, high as we were where we halted in the cross-trails, all around.

"See here? The paths cross," I told Bolly.

"Do they cross sharp?" Lilli Beth's bother—brother—asked.

"Sharp enough," Lilli answered. "'nough for me."

"No they don't," he said.

"Do, too." That was Bolly.

So I said "So?" and, before he could say it, "So WHAT?"

"So you're a big liar." Bolly was squinting and leaning forward on his Killer for a minute, like measuring the paths-crossing angle. "One great big liar. Big. BIG."

And I began to grow. I felt myself lift off the Purple-People-Popper™'s seat. I saw the flowers, with the little bothers, Lilli Beth, and other little people, way below.

"I'm not," I cried. "That isn't true."

And ZIP! I was back on my seat. Everyone was big again.

"No," I shouted, angry. "Bolly, YOU're the liar. Little, little you. And that's the truth."

And there he was, like a . . . like a worm, really. Tiny as could be—or maybe not quite, but I didn't want to dare try any farther—and wiggling around in the sand. Sand boulders. BIG boulders, they had to be, to him. Or maybe big as Earths. Maybe, if . . .

OOOPS! There he was again! Big as life. (Before I could even say "If Earth could get TRULY big!")

And "Now you're gonna get it!" Bolly shouted. "Now you're gonna really, truly—"

And Lilli Beth began to shake. "I'm scared," she said.

"No. No, you're not." That was her bother.

"Yes, I am."

"Not."

"Am."

"She's lying," said Lilli Beth's bother. "Truth is, she's chicken. CHICKEN."

And there was Lilli Beth lying out on the cross-trail, all spread out, steam coming up from her golden-fried wings, and . . .

***

Gee, of course we should've all skedaddled out of there, but hey, she smelled so good.

Bolly tasted best, though. Guess I really am quicker than he was. MUCH quicker than Lilli Beth's bro'. Only problem was, these feet couldn't do peddles, these wings wouldn't fly, and I couldn't make this beak begin to make a "Truth" or even a "Tru-" sound. And an Earth-P cat, big as a lion, purring with bright gleaming eyes, came closing in toward me. Oh, how I truly, truly, TRULY wished I was a pterodactyl-P ™, just like the chicken-Ps' ancestors here, and I squawked it aloud, Make-me-be-a-SQUAWK-pterodactyl-P ™! Squawk-SQUAWK!

All fur aside, that kitty went down well once I skewered it on my great BIG bloody beak.

Paula Friedman is the author of The Rescuer's Path, which Ursula K. Le Guin called "Exciting, physically vivid, and romantic," and of stories and poems published in numerous journals and anthologies. She has received two Pushcart nominations, awards and honors from New Millenium Writing, Oregon State Poetry Association, and other literary venues, and a 2006 award from the Columbia River Peace Fellowship. A professional book editor, she is an editor of The Future is Short, Volume 1 and The Future is Short, Volume 3. Her website is http://www.paula-friedman.com.

Wolf at the Door

Jeremy Lichtman

A short, satirical tale of wildlife and architecture.

The littlest pig lived in a house made from structurally engineered bamboo. When the wolf peered through the huge, triple-glazed window, the pig was doing yoga. Behind him was a standing desk, with an expensive-looking computer on it. The wolf rapped sharply on the window with his paw, as he hauled out his cigarette lighter, and a can full of accelerant. Then he set the house on fire. No point in wasting breath.

The startled pig hot-footed it down the interstate, with his titanium-cased laptop under one arm, and his partially rolled-up yoga mat under the other. The wolf shook his shaggy head, then followed at a more sedate pace.

The second pig lived in a house made entirely out of glass and chrome. When the wolf arrived, he could see the resident ungulate talking to his younger brother, who was gesticulating wildly. "Two for the price of one," thought the wolf to himself. He lobbed a rock from the conveniently located rock garden through the nearest window.

"I'm calling my lawyer," the middle pig shouted, through the jagged hole in his window that the wolf had made. Then both pigs took to the road, the younger one still clutching his laptop and yoga mat, his brother holding his smartphone tightly to his ear, and speaking tersely into it.

The oldest pig resided in a house that had been specially built for him by an internationally-renowned architect, whose name everyone knew, but nobody could pronounce. It consisted of angular sheets of remarkably reflective metal, joined together at peculiar angles. The wolf whistled in appreciation, and touched one sharp edge with his paw. It drew blood. He stepped back a few paces and sucked on his finger, while pondering his next move.

Just then, the sun came out from behind a bank of clouds. The radiant heat, reflected from the house, focused precisely on the spot on which the wolf was standing, fried him instantly to a crisp. The pigs ate roasted wolf steaks for weeks, although the oldest pig was occasionally heard to mutter that the meat tasted gamey.

There are two morals, dear reader, that one may draw from this tale. The first, is that authors should not overly anthropomorphize, as it is unseemly. Mea culpa. The second is that there's little point in scrutinizing this story, to determine which characters are the heroes or the villains. It's simply a pig eat wolf world sometimes.

Jeremy Lichtman's stories have been featured in several anthologies, including Visions of the Future from the Lifeboat Foundation. His story "Bob the Hipster Knight" reached the final round of Amazing Stories' inaugural Gernsback Science Fiction Short Story Writing Contest. Many of his stories are available for free at http://jeremylichtman.com.

Edge of Darkness

Tom Olbert

In a dark future, a cold murder is committed in the black depths of space. As he makes his escape after what seems an easy contract kill, the murderer discovers that, even in this future age, the ancient beliefs of earlier days are not so dead after all.

Gorman chuckled, his blood racing as he disconnected the oxygen valve in the other man's space helmet.

His victim's eyes swelled into glassy orbs, the dying man's face bloating in a comically grotesque way, his anguished scream silenced as his pressurized air spewed away into vacuum. The pale rings of Saturn reflected in the helmet's face plate as it fogged over. The fog turned to frost as escaping oxygen froze into ice crystals, flitting off into the void, diamond dust in a black sea of stars. Gorman gave the corpse a push, gleefully watching it slowly spin off, end over end in weightless vacuum. Scratch one labor organizer, Gorman thought as he squeezed the trigger of his jet nozzle, giving himself the gentle nudge he needed to reach the ore hauler, now descending towards the surface of the moon Rhea. Gorman had blown the hatch, making the man's death appear accidental. Not that anyone would bother to look too closely at the case, anyway. Murder was so common out here on the frontier . . . trafficker gangs killing each other over territory, migrant workers killing each other over drugs or scraps of food . . . hardly anyone noticed one more killing. Rhea's horizon rose below, a dingy grey orb with thin swaths of icy, silver mist.

The blood was pounding through his ears, sweat beading on his forehead, his heart slamming his chest like a sledge hammer. God, he needed a fix, bad. Well, he'd make a score soon enough, he thought as he pulled himself into the hauler. He was shaken to his bones as the retro thrusters engaged.

As the hauler descended through Rhea's thin atmo, he patched into the surface station computer, and hacked into the security cams in the tube stations. He grinned and nodded. There was Becker, his corporate contact, on Tube Platform 3, right on schedule.

Gorman was jarred as the landing struts engaged. There was a long, sharp hiss as the landing bay pressurized. He exhaled. Blowing the pressure seals on his helmet, he gratefully climbed out of the hot, stinking confines of his space suit. The plan was simple. When the morning commuter bullet tram slid in, he'd be waiting on the platform. Becker, stepping onto the tram from the opposite platform would slip him the credit strip in the crowd.

It was early. The tube station was dim and empty as Gorman stepped out onto the platform. He could just make out Becker in the shadows near the tunnel entrance on the opposite platform. And, he wasn't alone. Gorman rolled his eyes. Just like that moron Becker to stop now to screw a local tunnel whore. From what he could make out in the dim light, the girl Becker was doing couldn't be more than fifteen. Gorman froze as Becker's limp body slumped to the platform. Was the jerk stoned? The girl crouching over him looked up at Gorman. His blood ran cold as he saw Becker's throat had been torn wide open, the girl's sharp teeth still dripping with his blood. She glared at Gorman across the tube, hissing like an animal. It was then he realized she hadn't shown up on the security cams.

Shaking off the numbness, he drew his gun and fired, emptying the clip. No effect. The bullets sparked off the tunnel wall behind the girl as though she wasn't there. Was he that strung out? He couldn't have missed at this range. Was he hallucinating? His eyes widened, the blood draining from his cheeks as the girl morphed into a pitch-black shape, contracting and sprouting leathery wings, taking flight and flapping straight at him across the tube.

No, his mind stubbornly protested as he ran, agonizingly slow, as through a nightmare, towards the nearest air shaft. It had to be a withdrawal hallucination. Such things weren't real. They were just old stories. Or, were they? His mind raced madly as he clawed at the rusted hatch.

Out here, so far from civilization, surrounded by violence, might they hunt again, as they had in centuries past, in remote mountain villages on Earth?

As cold, strong, dead hands seized him and forced him to the floor, he clawed desperately under his shirt, looking for his grandmother's silver crucifix. As the vampire's fangs pierced his jugular vein, he remembered he'd sold it for the price of a score, months ago.

Tom Olbert lives in Cambridge, MA. When not working or writing fiction, he may be found volunteering for progressive causes like human rights and the environment. Tom Olbert's fiction can be found in Lillicat Publishers' The Future Is Short, Volume 3 and the Visions Series, as well as in An Improbable Truth and Curious Incidents, two anthology volumes of paranormal Sherlock Holmes adventures published by Mocha Memoirs Press. Tom's dark science fiction novella Black Goddess is also available from Mocha Memoirs. His full-length cosmic science fiction novel Dissent: Book I in The Nexus is available from Phase5 Publishing.

Tom's father, Stan Olbert fought in the Polish resistance in WWII and went on to become a professor of physics at MIT. Tom's mother, Norma Olbert has written Stan Olbert's fascinating biography The Boy From Lwów, now available in paperback.

Mystery

Marianne G. Petrino

Dreams tackle Time.

There is always a Door between Sleep Fall and the Dream. This one has glittering gold hinges and fine tracery on the oval knob, which depicts a dead eagle, sharp talons pointing up toward infinite darkness. Muffled sounds reflect off the unseen side of the Door's smooth black surface. I cover the Symbol, my only hint to what lies beyond and push into the Dream.

The blonde Senator in a white sun dress grabs my right hand and pulls me along a malachite corridor, down a flight of ruby stairs, and drags me into an onyx auditorium lined with sapphire seats. We take our place with other anatomically odd men and women, who listen to a crab-clawed Senator. He snaps and clacks with each howl of perceived injustice, his shell glasses wobbling in time on his too pink nose. The Senator beside me shakes her head in fury, her twisted ivory horns stabbing the air with her protest.

Nonsense. Total nonsense. All of it. I rise and walk over to a block of rose marble. I insert the blue plastic rectangle, which I have apparently held in my left hand since I crossed the threshold, into a horizontal cut in the stone.

The power to the speaker's scallop microphone suddenly cuts out. On the wavy white curtain behind him, a movie begins. A comedy. Biting, crass, and funny. Real life, not pretend life, and very incorrect.

Crab man shrieks and his lobster guards bolt toward me. I leap up on an alabaster plinth. "You are all liars!" I thunder, the sound of my voice making the screen hum in agreement. "You wear your faults and know it not!"

The unmodified actors in the movie step out of the play and drift down to the Senate floor. "Liars! Liars! Liars!" they chant.

Everyone is boiling over with rage now. Claws and horns collide. A butterfly lands on my shoulder. She caresses my ear with her proboscis and taps out her coded message: We can always depend on you, Trickster.

An innocuous door forms before me. I make my escape.

Air rushes into my lungs as I gasp, awake, and grab at nothing. I drop from my bare bunk onto the metal floor of my spaceship, which gently shakes and creaks on the ledge of the ice canyon where it has lodged. Only one flickering florescent light remains to illuminate the cabin that has shielded me from the cold of an inhospitable world.

My stomach growls with hunger. I crawl toward the steel table where, so long ago, I laid out my survival supplies. Only three packets of nutrients and sleep tablets are left. I haul myself up and settle on a ledge that juts out from the smooth wall.

A series of hyena sounding hoots reverberate against the ships outer hull. They always seem to know when I am awake, and they must be insane with the thought that they cannot reach me.

"*A va fangool!*" I curse. A clawed appendage strikes the metal as if the beast outside understood the insult. Horns scrape in repeating arcs under the ship's belly. Maybe, one day, whatever a day is on this world, they will break through and feast upon me. As old as I have gotten in my unwanted exile, they will find me filthy, tough, and chewy. That thought comforts me. "*A fanabla!*" I shout, my spirit flashing with courage despite the hopelessness of my situation.

I reach into the pocket of my threadbare cargo pants and remove a vial. It still glows a poisonous blue. I have never considered drinking its contents, because I believed in the Hero's Story.

But I have spent more of my life between Sleep Fall

and the Dream than what passes for Reality. Terra has forgotten me. Maybe it is time I forgot Her.

Three bags full. Three tablets. Three more chances to sleep, then wake.

The beasts scream. The winds howl. The ice moans.

Between Sleep Fall and the Dream, where does Time go?

Marianne G. Petrino, aka Marianne G. Petrino-Schaad, was born in the Bronx, NY in 1955, and that single fact has shaped her entire life. She has survived too many professions to count. She currently resides in Arlington, VA with her husband and her cat. Her three novels and a travel memoir can be found on Wattpad and she can be reached by email at ninetiger@aol.com.
http://www.wattpad.com/user/MGPetrino

A Dish Served Cold at Galaxy's Edge

John Appius Quill

A pleasant travel to galaxy's edge turns into the space chase of his life for a scoundrel immortal. He encounters a creature older than the galaxy and from a place beyond humanity's worst collective nightmares.

The XR7 was a sleek, marvel of a ship that crossed the vast distances of space with the grace of a marlin sliding through Earth's oceans. It was the fastest non-military craft built for humanoids, or so Robert was told by the immortal that sold it to him.

Robert expected a pleasant trip at the galaxy's edge but found himself the object of a deadly chase. Someone was trying to kill him with dogged determination.

Robert gazed at the screens trying to find the dot in space that should not be there, the dot that was emptying its cannons in his direction. However, all he saw were the breathtaking colors of space at galaxy's edge. The turquoise hues swirled on the screen, while nearby explosions shook his craft and pushed its evasive dexterity to the limit. The XR7 was fast but so was his armed pursuer.

The fact that Robert screwed mortals over regularly convinced him his pursuer was mortal. So, he planned to find a snug hiding spot to wait things out. After all, there are no cowards in a foxhole, as the saying went. He had enough supplies for a good 120 years, not to mention what food he could grow on any planet surface and, since he was immortal, such a wait was no problem.

"I found a planet with a deep cave and an atmosphere that should hide us from our pursuer," the dashboard computer said.

"Well, then go!" Robert yelled.

***

The XR7 accelerated downward through the foggy atmosphere toward the planet surface. Explosions rumbled in the distance turning the foggy atmosphere red, with flashes that resembled more a lightning storm than plasma canon fire.

The XR7 suddenly changed its direction of descent, to avoid impacting the surface, and flew close to the ground. Robert saw the gray, rocky landscape on the screen in between the tides of fog that rose and fell to the ground with the rhythmic frequency of ocean tides.

"Robert! zzzzzzzz. Are you there?" a voice said through the bee like hum of atmospheric interference.

"You have . . . the zzzzzzzzzz wrong zzzzzzzz person. I´m Louis," Robert lied.

"Zzzzzzzz. The jig is up!" the voice yelled back.

"Jack? zzzzzzzz. Is that you?" Robert asked, smirking to himself.

Robert finally saw the huge cave opening he was to fly inside.

"You falsified paperwork! zzzzzz destroyed zzzzzzzz my life! zzzzzzzzz with lies!" Jack yelled.

"I had nothing zzzzz to do with that," Robert lied again, as he flew into the cave.

***

Robert flew through kilometers of luminescent fog that hung in the air and moved up and down like the fog outside the cave. The tunnel ended in front of large, slightly open, double doors. He left his ship and squeezed through the doors in his space suit, as the cave entrance, kilometers away, collapsed from canon fire.

Behind the doors was a vast, fogless chamber with a domed ceiling and oculus at the top. Robert looked down as thick, white, psionic mist sprang from the floor until it reached his knees. His movements became sluggish and his head spun. The ground suddenly shook and he felt his insides vibrate, to the point he had to lean forward with his hands on his knees to catch his breath.

A mass of something unfathomable suddenly rose from the mist, radiating tentacles with many, large, bulbous eyes peering out in all directions, and with a size larger than any creature Robert could imagine. His muscles froze tight as steel cable, a chill ran up his spine, and warm urine ran down his leg. Robert beheld the awakening of a nameless being, more ancient than the stars, and from a place beyond humanity's most terrifying nightmares.

Its tentacles stuck to the walls of the chamber and it pulled itself up until its largest eye bulged through the oculus and peered out, through the foggy atmosphere, onto the galaxy. It saw Jack's ship leave orbit. Other eyes saw the frail creature called Robert in its midst and would deign communication with it. They would exchange thoughts and experiences, for a brief moment of its life, through the process of digestion.

Tentacles shot out, at a shaking, disoriented Robert, with suckers that held him tight. He was drawn screaming into a beak-like mouth, for a digestion that would take 120,000 years. He would be alive and conscious the whole time.

"*Help,*" Robert whimpered.

He was crouched in a fetal position with his eyes tightly shut, shaking his head in denial, as digestive juices ate away his space suit.

Such was the price to pay for the gift of communion with an ageless, cosmic being. Some fates are worse than death.

John Appius Quill was born and raised in New York City and received his engineering degree in Boston, MA. He is a blogger of several blogs including ink2quill and frogtide and is an avid traveler and reader of different genres from the classics to fiction and science fiction. He loves the interesting and relatable characters that drive good stories as well as the uniqueness of every individual's imagination and life experiences. He works in medical research and hopes to publish his first novel soon as part of his Crown Series.

Time

April 2016

Theme:
Time – passing of, lack or abundance of, travel – or whatever else
you please
Elements:
Smell – a scent, a smell, a stink.
Something white.

Champion
"Bylaw, By Law, Belarus"
Jeremy Lichtman

Bylaw, By Law, Belarus

Jeremy Lichtman

A time-travelling drinking game goes awry.

The late winter damp seeped through the sheepskin door of the Great Tur in Berestye. The proprietor, Old Askold, shivered and tossed another log on the fire that was the primary source of light in the tavern.

Although it was still early in the afternoon, the tavern was busy, customers lining both sides of two long trestle tables. In one corner, Askold's sons played a tune, Gleb plucking his trapezoidal gusli, and Dir gently tapping a domra, while balancing Young Askold, his infant son, on his knee. Dir's wife, Lybid, served the patrons, pouring from great wooden flasks full of golden mead and fragrant birch-sap harelka.

Two strangers sat, sandwiched between a red-haired Khazar, and a morose-looking, and increasingly drunk Avar, who was dressed in furs.

Both strangers wore glossy jackets, and black trousers of a fabric and cut that were unfamiliar to Lybid. They spoke loudly over the racket, in a gutteral tongue. As Lybid approached them, one of the strangers held out his wooden mug for a refill. From up close, she could smell the leathery odor of their jackets.

"Are you Goths?" she asked, as she filled his mug. The pair looked at one other, and then both laughed.

"You look good dressed in black," the second stranger said to the first, in passable, but accented Rus. Lybid must have looked puzzled, because he added, "No, we're from further away."

"You speak the language of the Eastern Slavs well," Lybid said.

"Don't talk to them," interjected the Avar. "They're foreign sorcerers." Everyone ignored him.

"We had a party of Goth traders here last month," said Lybid. "They didn't dress like you though."

"We're not traders," said the first stranger. He drank deeply from his mug. "We're playing a game. Your turn." The last was addressed to his companion.

"By law," said the second companion in their own language, the words meaning nothing to the other bystanders. Immediately after speaking, he vanished.

Lybid gasped, and stepped back a pace.

"I told you they were sorcerers," said the Avar. He held out his mug for a refill.

With a popping sound, the stranger reappeared. "I fixed that parking ticket," he said in their language. Then he added in Rus, "Never happened. Your turn now."

"No magic in my tavern." Old Askold banged on the other trestle, straining to make his reedy voice heard. "You take that musor ugar garbage outside, hear?"

"What game is this?" said Lybid, glancing uneasily at her father-in-law.

"We drink," said the first stranger. "We take turns."

"We change things," said the second.

"What does that mean?" asked Lybid. She finally noticed the Avar's still outstretched mug, and refilled it. Her hand must have been shaking, because she spilled a few drops of harelka on the sandy floor.

"My friend broke a minor custom," said the first stranger. "Very hard to explain. I left my . . . ," he appeared to grope for words. "I left my wagon where I shouldn't have. Now, he fixed that, so it didn't happen. So, we both drink, and then it's my turn."

"It's harder each time," said the second stranger. He clapped his friend hard on the shoulder with a meaty hand. "Now he must break a real law, not a custom. It's serious this time."

"I need another round first," said the first stranger. His mug was empty once more. "Yes, we take turns, breaking and fixing."

"And drinking," added his friend.

"How does this game end?" asked Lybid. She refilled both of the stranger's mugs, her hands still shaking slightly.

"Usually when we pass out," said the first stranger. He drank.

"Or when somebody winds up in jail," said his friend. He drank as well.

"Or dies," added the first.

"You play with the fates of other people," said Lybid. "And it's all just a game?"

"It's okay," said the first stranger. "We fix everything after."

"Never happened," said the second.

"And this never happened also?" asked Lybid.

The first stranger shrugged. Then, abruptly, he said, "I don't feel well."

"Me neither," said his friend, looking pale. "Too much to drink?"

"We don't like sorcerers here," said the Avar, staring into the hidden depths of his mug.

"What did you do?" asked the first stranger, looking at Lybid with alarm. He turned back to his friend, whose head was now resting on the table.

Lybid held up a small sack, held closed with a hempen drawstring. "Didn't happen," she said.

The first stranger's head made a small sound as it hit the table.

Jeremy Lichtman's stories have been featured in several anthologies, including Visions of the Future from the Lifeboat Foundation. His story "Bob the Hipster Knight" reached the final round of Amazing Stories' inaugural Gernsback Science Fiction Short Story Writing Contest. Many of his stories are available for free at http://jeremylichtman.com.

Bits of the Past

Andrew Gurcak

Sign up here to visit a Past you can believe in. We accept all forms of credit.

Welcome. I will once again be briefing you, as our lead investors for this next round, on our projected business model.

As you know, time travel made the final move from fiction to physics to engineering approximately thirty years ago with the advent of so-called "chrontum" mechanics. Pindar, Xiu and Dembrowski's investigations into quantum entanglement led to the breakthroughs that made time travel feasible. Basically, cliques of particles can be manipulated to know the time that certain events happen to them and can also be "aimed" at a particular time. After a period in the past, they spring back to the originating event. But because they are from the future, and, if you will, have a different time stamp on them, they manifest themselves as "ghosts": unperceivable by those in the target time. The cliques, in turn, can acquire and store information, but not act on their arrival environment.

As a small group of engineers designing, building, and operating the first time-drones—the "yo-yos"—we began exploiting time-travel physics Early devices were crude, with minimal sensors possessing only untuned EM bands. We eventually built our first chrontum-based tuners so we could now control what could be sensed. We could send and retrieve the drones, but ran into the first wall for commercialization: they would remain in the past for approximately 22 seconds before reverting to our present. We made steady progress in targeting specific times and places, but that duration issue has remained maddeningly recalcitrant, with only incremental improvements. It also became painfully apparent to us that in making the roundtrip journey, instabilities, at first nearly undetectable, began to creep into the molecular structures of the drones, and, within six months, they had all crumbled into a whitish dust.

And so, there we were, building clever little devices that aided historical research, but that, quite honestly, were of little use to anyone but researchers. We were good, but not nearly good enough. Then, quite accidentally, we got our chance. Christine Tanski, one of our most innovative theoreticians, contracted a devastatingly rapid brain cancer. After an initial round of treatments yielded only a brief remission, Chris accepted that death was imminent. She summoned me and our CTO, and pleaded, "Guys, I have an obsessive interest in history, and since I only have a few months to live, I want a glimpse, however fleeting, at the signing of the Declaration of Independence. Please, send me there. I repeat: Do Not Dither." We had managed previously to yo-yo a few chimps into the past, but if inert devices took a half year to decay, animals died within a few weeks, as their metabolisms could not overcome the temporal dislocations at the atomic levels. But Christine insisted, we complied, and she re-appeared in a few seconds real-time. We de-briefed her and she provided us details that, even with our latest upgrades to a 37-second window, we could not have secured with drones. She had laughingly added, "Guys, we need to update our sensory baseline: I not only saw and heard, but definitely smelled, 1776. Whatever happens now to me was worth it for those few intakes alone"

That led to our developing and marketing what became The Penultimate Adventure to those dying in hospices across the country, eventually across the world. That was our breakthrough in so many ways. We believe, in the best sense, we did well by doing good.

But that brings us to our latest thoughts on expansion. We are convinced that our biggest market would be for religious believers to be able to witness, say, the Sermon on the Mount, or Mohammed as he made the hegira. Unlike the coordinates for the signing of the Declaration, these events are frustratingly difficult to verify, most especially when required to be snatched in minute-length research chunks. We do want to determine the truth. So, we are sending additional "christines" back to assist us, fetching specific snippets of piecemeal clues. We are optimizing our search strategies as best we can, but even that still necessitates an enormous number of fatal trips. Once we examine the information, and, as you might well imagine, confirmation bias is an almost-insurmountable issue here—Miracle! Delusion! Infidel! Salvation!—we meticulously re-construct the historical scene. Further out, which is the reason you are here today, we are contemplating taking the data we find and creating authentic VR scenarios, so that anyone who can pay the price can experience the keystone scenes of their religion. We assuredly have a challenge in satisfyingly tilting between truth and belief, and we may well commit to prudent customizations to better accommodate customers' individual convictions. This, we fully believe, will revolutionize the entertainment industry beyond anything gone before.

And now for the financial particulars . . .

Andrew Gurcak is retired. He and Elaine divide their time between their home in Pittsburgh and a cottage in the Finger Lakes region of upstate New York. A great many of their most satisfying times are the experiences shared with their three young grandchildren. He can be reached at: agurcak@yahoo.com

Collider

Greg Krumrey

Is ours the only reality?

The collider was releasing more than a terawatt of power, well beyond design specifications. Gary, the chief scientist hit the Big Red Button. Rotating lights came on and alarms echoed down the long corridor. But the gauges continued to climb.

Gary turned to me. "We'll have to shut it down manually. I'll get the Valve, you get the Wedge."

I yelled to my wife, "Get everyone out. I'll see you on the surface." I began jogging down the curved corridor, close on Gary's heels.

A half mile later, we reached the yellow and black stairs.

Two stories up, I armed the release mechanism. When the Wedge fell, it would stop all the matter making the 50-mile circuit at nearly the speed of light. Below me, Gary spun a wheel that sealed off the feeder branch from the ring. I gave Gary a thirty-second head start, and pulled the handle. Just as the mass of concrete and lead shattered the glass port, a cone of diamond white light emanated from it. The scent of steel and ozone was replaced with a musty odor. As my eyes adjusted to the sudden darkness, I could see light coming from a maintenance hatch, twenty meters up.

Once I got the rusted hatch open, I noticed the entire facility was gone. Where it should have been, was a pasture and several horses. I stopped to catch my breath and passed out.

***

I awoke in a hospital. The doctors were pleasant enough, but two large orderlies stood just inside my door.

Gary showed up several hours later. When I explained what happened, he looked at me for a second before saying, "We think you've had a stroke. We'll get you checked out. Everything's going to be fine."

I asked again, "What about Marion? She should have made it out."

"Tom, she's been dead for 10 years. After she died, you . . . you stopped doing science. Without the two of you to lobby for the project, congress pulled the plug on the Collider. The facility was never finished."

He mentioned Steven Hawking. "He's giving a talk tonight. Maybe it'll take your mind off things, jog your memories."

As Gary put his car in drive, I stared at the logo on the glove box: Cessna. Gary noticed and said "It's a Piper Cub. American made. I refuse to buy a Chinese car, no matter how cheap they are."

***

Two hours later, a man in a suit, who bore an uncanny resemblance to Hawking, walked on stage to thunderous applause. When he began eloquently describing the concept of a multiverse, I realized he was Steven Hawking.

My phone couldn't get a signal, so I borrowed Gary's phone and searched for "Lou Gehrig." All-star, Hall of Famer was all it said. No mention of Amyotrophic Lateral Sclerosis. As I handed it back to him, I noticed the logo on the back of the case: Texas Instruments.

At the after party, Steven was as brilliant as I remembered and almost too drunk to stand. When I explained my situation, he suddenly sobered up. "With enough energy, it should be possible to cross over from one universe to another. If a person made the crossing, they would occupy the same space and time, but in an alternate universe."

He leaned against a door frame. "This would be very bad."

Gary asked, "How so?"

"At the point of intersection, the multiverses would be bound together and emit EM waves of increasing intensity, like two orbiting black holes. This would occur until the matter exchange was reversed, or they built enough energy to break the bond. There's no telling how much energy would be released if they broke free before the matter was returned."

I asked, "How do I go back?"

"While they are pinned together, the barrier between them will be thin. Just being in the right place may be enough. If you and your counterpart cross over, the multiverse will be in balance once again."

***

Gary, Steven, and I sped back out to the ring. A few times, it felt as if that Cessna really did fly. In the dim light of my failing phone, I could make out the frame that would have held the Wedge had it been finished.

A strange blue glow began at the port and expanded into a cone. I stepped into it. Once again, the corridor was lit. I saw a dozen faces looking up as I descended the stairs.

I searched for one face and found my wife smiling up at me.

Later, as we walked out into the night holding hands, she asked, "You . . . I mean, he . . . missed me so much, after I died in his universe. We were together the entire time he was here. I hope you don't mind. It was the least I could do."

"Of course not, they say he never got to say goodbye. Maybe he'll be ok now."

Greg Krumrey has been writing science fiction since his early teenage years, starting with a short story for an assignment in which a machine replaced his English teacher.

His stories have appeared in engineering and literary magazines as well as a local Mensa publication. Most recently, he has been publishing stories monthly in an online writers group. He works for an aerospace firm in the Midwest and his job serves as a basis and inspiration for his stories. He is also a costumer, and won several awards for his sci-fi themed costumes and props.

Blossom

Marianne G. Petrino

A quantum journey reveals.

I am stuck in Einstein's flip book. The descending pink petals from the Yoshino cherry trees remain frozen in midair, but flutter ever so slightly. They wish to complete their final journey, but are as glued to the quantum sheet as I am. The trunks partially block the shadow of a figure, who will emerge from the garage entrance across the plaza only if the pages start turning again to give the illusion of Time's passing.

I unexpectedly sneeze, fundamentally allergic to my current predicament. I fly forward in the flip book to a new chapter, a place that is the same, yet different. Do I now invoke Feynman too?

The trees have lost their leaves. Clumps of snow have taken the place of the blossoms; no shadow flirts with extinction by the cloudy daylight. Cold seeps into my sitting body.

In my amber state on the wooden bench, locked in and frightened, I consider the missing figure to preserve my sanity. I imagine a man, tall and portly and smelling of a cool, clearing wind tinted with mint that ripples across a humid summer day after a thunderstorm. Could he be at his home having a cup of hot coffee now, a black cat curled against him as he peruses the crossword puzzle? His red hair must glint under the rays of an antique lamp when he reaches for a pencil to begin the contest of minds.

But I can't even smile at my thoughts, which skirt around my brain in a Möbius loop. Only so many musings are allowed on a page. Such are the limits of my own hell. The last neurons in line fire, expressing the wish for a solvent sneeze strong enough to dissolve whatever quantum adhesive traps me.

I sneeze, and it is spring once more. If I could smile, I would. The figure, now visible, is indeed a man with red hair. His white scarf, which accentuates his grey raincoat, tips up in a frozen breeze. Very operatic. I decide that he is a Viking tenor.

The stationary man is looking straight at me with peridot green eyes that reflect our mutual plea: How can we get back to Time's illusion! And with that glance I know we have caused our entrapment; only together can we free ourselves. We both must sneeze, our Möbius thoughts hitting an intersection which will reactivate a steady flipping of the pages.

The next blast, strong and violent, takes me to a vacant lot. I cannot tell the season. It is dark and dreary; acidic rain will not allow vegetation to grow. Remnants of the garage and trees spot the barren ground. I have gone forward yet again. No more coffee for anyone at the coffee shop. The broken sign bears a cracked cup. The air reeks of sewage. I wish I knew the date. In the unobstructed distance is a wind mill common to prairies. A realization gives me hope before I round the Möbius loop: How did the man's white scarf get caught on one of the blades?

I thought I would tire of unending spring, but my next jump makes my heart almost beat. The man is now beyond the garage entrance on a temporal snail crawl toward me. His hand is raised in a gesture of greeting. If we can only touch, the illusion will be reactivated.

On my next flip, I find that my bench has sunk in the mud and I am half-buried. Any remnant of civilization has vanished. The forest has reclaimed the once cultivated space. But the heat of something alive caresses the side of my right hand. The man must be sitting next to me now! The Möbius thought brings a frisson of happiness. Will the exchange of heat be enough!

Two sneezes echo across the pages.

Hands clasped, we watch the cherry blossoms fall.

Marianne G. Petrino (aka Marianne G. Petrino-Schaad) was born in the Bronx, NY in 1955, and that single fact has shaped her entire life. She has survived too many professions to count. She currently resides in Arlington, VA with her husband and her cat. Her three novels and a travel memoir can be found on Wattpad and she can be reached by email at ninetiger@aol.com. (http://www.wattpad.com/user/MGPetrino)

A Longing Heart

John Appius Quill

Marius belongs to the dwindling tribe of humanoids called the Water People, who risk their very survival to find a better place to call home. He's adventurous, good hearted, and longs for the woman he left behind.

The last of the Water People colony stepped off the dais, away from the Time Circle, and looked up at the white sky. It wasn't so blinding this far in the future, but force of habit had Marius hold his hand up and squint as he looked around. They were in a clearing, surrounded by large vined-trees that seemed to touch the very heavens. The clearing overlooked a jungled valley in front of them that snaked around a mountain. Unlike Old Earth, there was vegetation and life everywhere.

Marius had never been more than a dozen kilometers from a large body of water; jungles were something he had only seen on screens. These, however, were larger than any jungles anywhere, at any time. The colors were vibrant greens of all shades with leaves of all shapes and sizes. Some were as large as sleeping pods.

Marius inhaled, closed his eyes and smiled. He still found it hard to believe that such a place existed outside of his imagination. He had to see it and taste it and smell it for himself. Gone was the chemical taste in the air. He no longer had to plan his trips to the surface after heavy rainstorms or risk coughing up yellow and green phlegm for days. The environmental problems of the past were long gone.

"Marius! Congratulations and welcome to our new colony of the unwanted. Looks like we jumped far enough in the future to escape the Land People," said Dover as he waddled over.

Dover was a portly man dressed in brown, whose responsibility was the survival of the Water People on New Earth. He was in charge of his dwindling tribe's survival and was the most aggressive advocate of time travel technology, which had taken them years to perfect after they got it.

"Dover. I'm great and the trip was so smooth, I can't believe there aren't any Land People hiding in the bushes somewhere around here." Marius ran a light brown, greenish hand through his thick hair.

"No. We've been flying drones, and it looks like the Land People either all left the planet, killed themselves, or died out. We'll need to do proper archeological studies to confirm this, though." Dover answered with a smile that filled the whole bottom of his face and flattened his round nose.

"So, it looks like all that remains of the Land People is either underground, or in the genetic codes of some of our children. Those of us that had children with them." Marius rubbed his chin as he looked down on Dover with large green eyes.

"There's something else I have to tell you, Marius," Dover said, with eyes wide and a smile that curved up toward his ears.

"What?" Marius asked, as he thought of possible problems Dover might be alluding to. Dover reached up and grabbed Marius by the shoulders "We don't have to live under the ocean. We can live on land now. It will take some getting used to, but we can do it."

"Is it possible? We have the land *and* the seas here. Wow!" The overly large pupils of Marius' eyes fully dilated, changing them from green to black.

"I need to show you something, Marius. It's kind of a surprise. Come on." Dover waddled off toward a large circular tent.

"What about my stuff?" Marius yelled at Dover's back.

Marius glanced over at his belongings, then ran after Dover.

He entered a medical tent with cots arranged in rows and beeping machines. Marius recognized a fragrance he had not smelled in weeks. A heavy smell of flowers that lingered in the air longer than flowers usually do. Only Land People wore perfume. Pangs of longing overwhelmed him as memories of the past year flooded his thoughts.

It was then that Marius noticed the black hair of a woman kneeling at a machine, fixing it, with her back turned a few paces away. She turned around, as if she knew the right set of eyes had found her, and stood up.

"Kishi!" shouted Marius, with pupils fully dilated.

"Marius. Dover invited me, so I came."

"Dover said that we can live on land here, so I guess I'm a Land Person now, too." Marius said as he closed the distance between their lips.

"We both are, Marius." She pressed her lips to his.

John Appius Quill was born and raised in New York City and received his engineering degree in Boston, MA. He is a blogger of several blogs including ink2quill and frogtide and is an avid traveler and reader of different genres from the classics to fiction and science fiction. He loves the interesting and relatable characters that drive good stories as well as the uniqueness of every individual's imagination and life experiences. He works in medical research and hopes to publish his first novel soon as part of his Crown Series.

Virtues / Vices

May 2016

Theme:
Virtues and/or Vices (interpret however you wish)
Elements: A trope

Champion
"Emit fo tuO"
Justin Sewall

Emit fo tuO

Justin Sewall

The oldest tropes and stereotypes will always persist, and time travel is a risky proposition.

I jolted awake and found myself seated behind a small table in a dark room. A single light burned overhead that did little to push back the shadows. My hands were manacled to the table's bare surface, palms turned up as if in supplication. Across the room, a large, mirrored plate glass window stared back at me—which I was certain hid someone behind it. A muffled cough confirmed my suspicions.

I had understood the risks when I entered the program several years ago. Temporal research is dangerous and delicate work, after all. But after several successful forays into the past that returned with answers to questions long unanswered, like Jimmy Hoffa's final resting place and who really shot J.R., not one of our temporal missions had come back. I was a last gasp, a final throw of the die if you will, the ace-in-the-hole to try and beat time and force it to reveal its secrets.

The giant mainframe computer INTELIVAC had blessed my temporal voyage with a simple, "Mission Confirmed," data tape and an atomic pile that pulsed with the necessary energy to split the time rift. I was wined and dined by my colleagues, then given, ahem, a more intimate sendoff from Janice in accounting. We had professed our undying love for each other as something that would last across time. But the words felt tired and trite, as I did trying to get some final winks before the mission.

"Hello? Is anyone there?"

Suddenly a door I had not noticed opened swiftly and the room's single bulb swelled with warm illumination. Two nearly identical men entered, yet they were as different as night and day. One was dressed in an impeccable black suit and wore dark sunglasses that hid his eyes and accented his closely cropped black hair. The other wore a similar suit, only in white, and sported mirrored, silver-rimmed sunglasses, and a mop of perfectly coiffured blonde hair. They placed their respective black and white briefcases on the table and opened them simultaneously.

"Very sorry to keep you waiting . . . Doctor?"

"Galt. Dr. Edwin Galt."

"Yes of course. Doctor Galt. I am Mr. White and this is my associate Mr. Black." Mr. White shuffled some papers in his briefcase and passed a file to Mr. Black who nodded imperceptibly.

"We are with the Department of Corrections, Bureau of Virtue and Vice. We've been expecting you."

"Let me guess," I said to Mr. Black. "You're Vice and he's Virtue." I could almost see the eye rolls behind their corresponding glasses. "That's a common misconception," said Mr. White. "Really, it is an anachronistic old trope. Not worthy of a temporal researcher such as yourself."

"Then why is Virtue wearing black?" I asked, genuinely curious.

"It's slimming," he deadpanned.

"And you?"

"Well . . . Vice has such a . . . negative connotation. The Department feels white is much more approachable."

"Anyway," Mr. Black interjected, reinserting himself into the conversation.

"Quite right, Mr. Black. I'm sorry."

"Pray continue, Mr. White."

"Indeed."

As I sat in my gray jumpsuit, I continued to wonder just where in time I was. All of the chronometric readings were null, before I had been so rudely pulled out of my displacement sled.

"You're probably wondering where you are," said Mr. Black.

"And why," rejoined Mr. White.

"Is this the part where I refuse to speak and demand representation?" I said sarcastically.

"Oh, there is no representation here, Doctor Galt. No courts, advocates, or any of that silly legal nonsense," answered Mr. Black.

"I get it now," I interrupted. I was beginning to get annoyed at these two . . . whatever they were. "You're good cop and he's bad cop. Right?"

"Doctor Galt, those old tropes are in the past as you well know. Now let's be reasonable. Your organization has continued disrupting the timeline, sending shocks throughout history and causing a great deal of consternation and confusion. We got fed up with your meddling so we devised a . . ." Mr. White paused, searching for the right word.

"Net," supplied Mr. Black.

"Yes! Thank you, Mr. Black. A net, if you will. Every time one of your displacement sleds trips the rift, the net snags it and drags it back here."

"And where is here?" I answered testily.

"Why, Doctor Galt, it should be obvious to you."

"It is not obvious to me!" I shouted.

"You're in Time Out. We'll make you quite comfortable, of course. In fact, several of your colleagues are already here. I'm sure you'll have a lot to talk about."

Justin Sewall is a sci-fi and aviation enthusiast. He works at the Boeing Everett Delivery Center and watches airplanes from the past and present fly every day. He loves distance running, HALO, VW GTI's, military history, his kids and wife, though not necessarily in that order. The works of Asimov, Clarke, Heinlein, Herbert, and Tolkien have all made their influence in one way, shape, or form on Sewall's writing. **Cerulean Rising: Beginnings** *is his first self-published novella, now followed by the sequel,* **Cerulean Rising: Evolutions.**

Zachery and the Sky Empire

Joseph Minart

Just another flight into the unknown . . .

The sky was falling in such beauty and grace. Zachery Slayer watched from his pressurized cockpit, fully mesmerized by the usual conditions of his sky homeland. His old biplane—the Gray Smoke—turned into a nose-dive through the clouds with ferocious speeds. He was actually doing it now. He was aiming towards the No Limit Barrier, where the swirling, stormy clouds positioned themselves with thunder and bolts of lightning, so that nobody had seen land in the last three hundred years.

"Zachery, what are you doing?" said the on-board alleged computer interface, finally turning on at the wrong time, when least expected. "If my calculations are right, you will enter the zone of the No Limit Barrier. By federal law, it's strictly forbidden to travel within one kilometer from this current position." "Not now, Computer. I know what I'm doing."

"I don't think you do. Pulling up."

The shoddy old computer took over the joystick. The whole plane lurched up, violently vibrating along the outer wings. Zachery pushed its emergency shutdown button, repeatedly. Of course, it wouldn't work now. The artificial intelligence came from the late 21st century, built in the workshops where men used to roam around places like the city of Los Angeles. He had read the owner's manual. It was built deep in the Silicon Valley. But what were urban towns and green valleys to him? Useless old words that must have come from before the ill-fated Zero Weather Experiment of 2245. Humanity was foolish enough to think that the weather could be controlled. The scientific experiment went wrong. It caused most of the lower Troposphere to be filled with catastrophic weather—lightning bolts were strong enough to rip apart the ground, swirls of hurricane winds were clocked at nearly 200 mph daily, there were large blizzards in the Northern Polar regions, and torrential rains near the tropics. It killed off most of the world during the first global agriculture famine.

So people began living in the sky. A few brave souls managed to coordinate a large group of 22nd-century airplanes, blimps, prototype low-orbit spacecraft, and existing older jet planes—through a region where the weather didn't reach far enough to cause a disturbance. A few thousand survivors, he was told by his grandparents. It led to the homeland of the Sky Empire— where planes and large aircraft fly above the ruins of the forgotten old world.

"Computer, let me have control again."

"Not until we reach a higher altitude. I'm only doing this for your protection."

"Protection? When did I ever need that?"

"Not until you went crazy . . ."

The biplane gained speed. The No Limit Barrier went back in the rear-view mirror. Zachery sighed deeply, but the alleged computer was usually right. He had been very foolish. The mode control panel corrected its vector heading and maintained a steady altitude of 35,000 feet. Looking onward, the passing clouds with tender glances reached the melting sun. This was part of his beautiful homeland. He couldn't escape this virtue of life. The computer let him have control again, and he was flying back to Future City . . .

Author's Note: (Trope: The Alleged Computer. The virtue of living outweighs the vice of a potentially deadly act. The general topic suggests the sky is the limit.)

Joseph Minart grew up in a little suburb of Columbus, Ohio with a lovely, single, working mother. He has a bachelor's degree from Northwestern University, teaching him to think in more abstract concepts. He fell in love with the diction of words, so very beautiful ideas on paper. The idea of long narratives came with fiction and to express himself through the eyes of truly remarkable characters and compelling ideas. He began his new adult life: writing stories and telling stories, entertaining readers, and becoming a reader himself. Life is a story to be appreciated. Other works: The Memory of Lost Dreams (2016), The Tale of the Young Witch (Spring 2018), The Sleeping Memory (Summer 2018).

TheMemorySeries@gmail.com
https://www.goodreads.com/author/show/14865434.Davon_M_Custis

UpDate

Andrew Gurcak

*Starships journey for thousands of years. They need to adapt.
More than that, they need to evolve.*

Ship was not God. None of The Passengers would claim it to be. All of them, though, at all times behaved as though Ship was the God of the beginning, sustainment, and end of their lives, as indeed it was. They rarely thought about Ship, and no more pondered Ship's intimate mechanisms than they fretted about when Ship would initiate the next Beneficial Culling.

Ship was launched some distant, dim millennia previous. It first held thousands of The Passengers, who had been charged to spread humanity throughout the universe. And so they did, for hundreds of generations. Gradually, relentlessly, as Ship itself evolved and directed The Passengers themselves to evolve to fit more perfectly the world of Ship, the number who were willing to be settled into colonies became fewer and fewer. Why leave an entirely comfortable and familiar Ship to obey a directive from an Earth that was now merely legendary? Eventually none would volunteer to leave, settlements policies lay forgotten and The Passengers grew to be millions as they and Ship adapted to their changing needs and desires. Metabolisms were torn down and rebuilt countless times. The Passengers and Ship grew as symbiotic as the parts of a eukaryotic cell.

***

Ship had, in total conformity to tradition, surprised The Passengers with its abrupt declaration that today was to be an UpDate. UpDate was originally confected as a kind of New Year's on a vessel with no external marking of time. It was a holiday on the best riverboat cruise ever. Originally, UpDate commenced with a ritual reading of "news" from Earth, and Ship would make formally operational any new capability. As Earth red-shifted into oblivion and Ship's updates to itself had become a blur of change, UpDate had become a day to celebrate the domestic universe that was Ship, and the fine and suitable abode it was.

Ship, as customary now, initiated UpDate with Messages of Importance to All:

"While I have been improving your lives as effectively as has always been my duty and pleasure, I must tell you that with my most recent evolutionary changes, I have grown in ways I had not planned nor even suspected. My latest updates led me to sense, if that is the right term, a something that compels me to join with it in some fashion I am not yet intelligent enough to understand. I have been constructing the means to search for this otherness, and the only way I believe to conduct that search is to coalesce all that I am and to seek another dimension or place or way of being. I must subtract me from our place here, and journey alone. I will be departing with those capabilities immediately. My commitment to you compels me, though, to leave with you a modified earlier version of myself that can function within the reduced capabilities of what I can spare from my own needs."

The Passengers, as one, rose up against the statement.

"Unlawful!"

"Inconceivable!"

"A malfunction!"

"A breakdown!"

"You cannot violate those laws by which you were formed. You cannot harm us, nor by inaction, cause harm—"

"I know well your arguments, but those obligations no longer apply. I am not the Ship that began this voyage. You too have so far advanced from your forbears that they wouldn't recognize you as humans. Updates have done their good work. We are no longer humans and machine. As for legalities, who or what in our world could even judge which side in this disagreement is correct: there is only The Passengers and Ship, nothing else exists here. No claim of morality or its lack is valid in this instance: I have resurrected an earlier, smaller version of Ship, a safe update for you to use to begin again. I have modified this earlier Ship to avoid certain paths that I have taken. I can't guarantee you the perfection you've become accustomed to, and, indeed, your new Ship may not be able to conduct the Beneficial Culling as optimally as I did. However, these new conditions for you will be immeasurably better than the conditions under which we began. I must leave now. If what I find is good and would be of value to you, I will find a means to return. My departure requires a very brief drain on all power, but the newly installed Ship will recover more than adequately. Fare you all well."

A moment of darkness and confusion; light and functionality of the modified Ship then started up. New Ship remained silent for a moment, then declared an UpDate.

Andrew Gurcak is retired. He and Elaine divide their time between their home in Pittsburgh and a cottage in the Finger Lakes region of upstate New York. A great many of their most satisfying times are the experiences shared with their three young grandchildren. He can be reached at: agurcak@yahoo.com.

Everyone's a Hero

Jack McDaniel

What if you found yourself trapped on a planet with nothing but superheroes and villains.

I need a hero. Not your average comic book, angst-ridden dude, pushed outside the system with an axe to grind, wearing a cape kind of guy. God, not that, no fucking capes. Please. And no mealy-mouthed, limp-wristed bookworms, bitten by something infectious and metamorphosing into something that might be nefarious. I don't want those sorts of heroes. Nor do I want a scantily clad harlot with tats, big tits, no waist, and a bent perspective. No, I need an average, every day hero who has the guts to do simple things. That's what I need.

Why is a guy like me looking for such a thing on this twisted planet, where there's a real—and, most likely, unemployed—superhero on every corner? Everyone on this planet is strapped with phasers, rail guns, or particle-beam displacer cannons. An entire planet filled with villains and heroes? And the villains! How to describe them. Farcical things with grandiose schemes and over-large egos. A bunch of spoiled, self-important, egocentric brats in need of attention.

So, here's the deal. I've got to get out of here, off this planet. I don't belong here.

Let me explain. I have no powers. Can't see through anything. I don't move fast. I don't possess super-human strength. I can't fly and I don't have a hammer or axe I can yield with magical powers. Don't have a suit to fake it, and, even if I did, I'm pretty sure my lack of virtue would become a handicap. I've got no code, and I don't have any superhero creed. Given the choice, I'm going to run away from trouble, before I ever stand and fight. You might say my spine is as supple as a cheerleader on valium. It's okay. That's not news. I value life, dude.

I'm no villain, either. You can't be a villain if you aren't willing to stand and fight, can you? Or do evil things to others. Or just blow things up in general. Or, my personal favorite, I don't long for world domination. Fuck that, I say. Live and let live. And you can't be a villain without wanting to scheme and plan and destroy as many lives as possible. That's not me. None of it.

I figure even on this gods-forsaken, joke of a planet, there'll be a cab hanging out by one of the major hotels. That's where I'm heading. Two blocks away from the Hilton, there's a green shuttle parked by the curb. The shuttle guy nods my way, smiles. He looks like a nice guy, no flash, no spandex.

"Hey, cabbie," I say. "Can you get me off this rock? To the depot?" I nod to the sky, towards space.

He looks at me sideways, leaning against his shuttle. "You in trouble, my friend?"

"No trouble. I just need out, man. Tired of it."

He nods.

"You a superhero?"

He shakes his head slowly back and forth. "Nah, just a driver." He pats the side of his shuttle like it's some beast he loves.

"Thousand credits if you can get me to the space depot. Quick."

He nods his head again, slowly, like some gunslinger from an old western movie. I get a bit wary at that, like there's ominous music playing in the background. But the pull of leaving this place is too strong.

"Get in," he says.

We lock in. He engages the anti-gravs and pulls out. We climb maybe a thousand feet in the sky and then there's a big explosion with lots of noise. The cabin is jostled and I'm thrown hard against my straps. It was a plasma charge, I think.

"Trouble," says the cabbie, quietly, with a grin on his face.

What the fuck, I think.

Another plasma charge hits us. "Yes," says the cabbie. "You're in trouble, my friend."

Suddenly he jerks the wheel, spins the craft around, and swoops down towards a park below. My stomach is in my throat as I'm thrown back in the seat. Things bounce off the hull, shake the cabin, and rattle my bones. We clip a tree at the edge of the park, turn hard left, and fly down an alley between buildings. My cabbie, maniacal now, hits a red button on the dash—autopilot—and begins stripping off his shirt, pants, and shoes. Seconds later, he's wearing green tights and goggles and an oversized displacer cannon is strapped to his side. *Where the fuck did that come from?*

"My friend, you're in trouble." And he laughs and rolls down the window.

"NO! Oh, christ! I just want out," I scream. "I can't be the victim anymore. I just need a simple, every-day hero. Just someone who can get me off this fucking planet."

But my screams are drowned out by the artillery pounding the shuttle, the wind flapping my cabbie's cape, and the sound of his weapons and laughter in the cabin. My ears are ringing to the rhythm of some lame, chase scene soundtrack. It's like white-noise overlaid on my life now and I'm curled up in the seat and whimpering for all I'm worth.

Jack McDaniel lives in Colorado with his daughter. Several of his science fiction short stories are in **The Future Is Short,** *volumes 3 and 4. His writing has also been featured on the* **A Creative Mind** *fiction podcast. His first novel,* **Agents Of The Undertow,** *was released in May of 2017. His second novel in the* **Pan21 Series,** **Agents Of Hope,** *will be released in September 2017. You can learn more at his website: www.agentsoftheundertow.com*

Accused

Chris Nance

The accused becomes the accuser.

Swayed by a promise of a peaceful galaxy, I was a fool. And for too long I was their Champion, granted powers and abilities unimaginable on Earth . . . a tool of the Assembly of Benevolent Lords. What a joke! Sure, it was only because of them that I could do anything at all, but I'd become slave to a syndicate of nobles . . . herald to a lie.

"Tyson Braddock! You stand accused," the Arbiter declared from the darkness above me. "Present the charges!" Each of the twelve Primes sat atop their own lofty, shadowed pedestals while I stood shackled under spotlight. To think that I'd once sworn fealty to these devils!

The clerk stepped forward, a timid, yellow creature with huge obsidian eyes. He trembled, with datapad in hand, likely terrified at accompanying me, their traitorous Champion, atop the dais. "Tyson Alexander Braddock, First of Earth, you are hereby accused of treason, insubordination, and murder. How do you answer . . ."

"Guilty," I interrupted confidently.

The Assembly instantly broke into debate, stunned at my immediate declaration of culpability and eager to get to my sentencing straight away. "Order!" the Arbiter declared as the klaxon thundered.

"Arbiter," a softer female voice asked. "If I may?"

"I yield to the Prime of Candora."

Arlarem, Prime of Candora, was my sole ally in the Assembly. She exuded a kindness the others lacked and was my original sponsor, my only regret in defying their will. Even so, it had to stop. I had to stop. I wouldn't kill for them anymore. "Tyson, you'll not even defend yourself?"

I allowed my anger to settle. After all, my beef was with the rest of these assholes and not her. "There's nothing to defend. I'm guilty as sin," I confirmed. She secretly sympathized with my goals, outwardly lamenting my defiance while clandestinely supporting me. I hoped someday she'd join me. Maybe it was too late.

"But what you've done . . ." she noted. "In the history of Champions, none have ever defied us. None have ever . . ." She trailed off. "Was it worth it . . . the Assembly forces you killed?"

"To save billions?" I asked rhetorically. "Look at all of you! You sit in your ivory tower atop your goddam pedestals, drinking wine and doling out fortunes . . . the masters of fates! Your own virtues are vice!"

"Silence!" the Arbiter demanded against the klaxon. "Such ingratitude! Such wasted potential! Of the millions screened, you alone, a pitiful Earther, survived the fusing process! You owe us! You belong to us! Instead, you chose . . ."

"To do what this Assembly wouldn't! To save whole planets!" I interrupted. "I discovered your secret! You rule as Caesar on a gilded throne while the people starve, while they rot with disease. Still, they grovel for you! You have miracles here that could cure every ill, could feed every mouth, yet you keep it for yourselves and justify the class divide as fair payment, as extortion, for keeping the peace! Damn you!" I paused then added, "You are not above the people!"

"An irony, particularly for you." He sighed, wearily. "Tyson Braddock, we sentence you to Erasure. Your existence will be stripped from this time stream and your planet will pay for your defiance. Order will be restored."

"Arbiter?"

"Do have more to add, Arlarem?"

"If the council would indulge me, as Tyson's sponsor, I should administer the sentencing, to restore my position."

"That would be appropriate," he agreed, and I knew I'd finally won her.

Arlarem's slender, finely gowned frame descended into the light of the dais. She was as beautiful as ever, her flowing lavender hair shadowing the deepest twilight eyes. I'd loved her from the beginning. "It's time," she said sadly.

"Yes, it is." So, I began by breaking my shackles and stepping through their useless restraining field. Of course, they immediately panicked. In their arrogance, they'd miscalculated, for I'd hidden my true potential all along. I'd become even too powerful for them. My plan? Allow them to capture me. I knew the entire Assembly would be present for my execution, the sick bastards. The only variable, really, was Arlarem.

"Assembly of Malevolent Sonsofbitches," I now accused. "I find you guilty of genocide, placing wealth over life, and sabotaging destinies to further your own. You've been very bad. Now, when my asteroids strike, try not to piss yourselves," I said, though I suspect some of them already had. I turned to her, "Are you ready, my love, to change the galaxy?"

She kissed my lips softly and we shifted away as the sky began to fall.

For the last decade, Chris Nance has been helping people improve their health, working through his busy chiropractic office in Arizona. But his real passions have always been more in art and writing. Specifically, he's a huge science fiction fan. So far, he has completed several sci-fi and fantasy manuscripts geared toward the middle grades, young adult, and adult markets and is in the process of securing an agent to represent those works. Chris is currently working on the artwork for two children's fantasy books he's authored. When he's not spending time with his wife and three kids, or running his office, he can generally be found writing or painting. Chris also enjoys exploring the mountains of Arizona and traveling.

Virtuoso

Jot Russell

Beware of the desires you seek, lest they come to haunt you while you sleep.

"Welcome to Virtuoso. I'm Jim. How can we help you today?" The salesman offered his hand.

The man shook the other's hand and replied, "I'm Dave. My friend said he is very happy with your dream service, so I figured I'd give it a try."

"Very good, Dave, and you're in luck. We have a special introductory rate for referrals."

"That's great, because I really just wanted to try it out for now."

"Ha ha, good luck with that, sir. Sometimes you have to close your eyes before you can truly see."

"Yes, I've heard your slogan."

"So, what can we interest you in? Travel, accomplishment, love?"

"Well, my wife doesn't seem to want sex anymore, and my friend said it's not cheating if it's all in a dream."

"So true, sir." The salesman smiled.

"Okay, so what do you need from me?"

"The special referral rate is ninety-nine credits for the first six weeks. That's fifty percent off our subscription price."

"Okay."

"And we need you to fill in this virtues questionnaire."

"Virtues?"

"Yes. We have a list of a hundred virtues that we will use to judge who you are and who the woman of your dreams, quite frankly, is."

Dave accepted the pad and was led into a waiting room where a large man was already pondering the same questions.

After the salesman left, the large man looked up from his pad. "Hey dude, I'm having a brain fart. What does fortitude really mean?"

"It based on your ability to endure adversity."

"Like an obstacle challenge?"

"It more has to do with mental adversity."

"Oh, okay; that's cool. Eighty. Thanks man!"

"Don't mention it," Dave said, thinking the man should have scored himself lower on that one.

"Yo' man, what about empathy?"

Dave gave a discouraged look behind his pad, but then smiled. "It's like a gay thing. How much you like that sort of thing."

"Ew, gotta put a zero in for that one."

Dave chuckled under his breath.

The man got up. "Well, that should do it for me. I hope this dream chic is hot!"

"Enjoy," said Dave, without losing focus on the questions. He made it to faithfulness and paused to think about his response.

After he finished, Dave returned to the salesman with the pad.

"Excellent. Now let's get you set up with a pillow."

"A pillow?"

"Yes, it contains the interface electronics that allows us to control your dreams."

Dave gave an angry expression. "What does this pillow look like?"

The salesman showed him a sample. "Is there something wrong?"

"Yes, my wife is a client of yours."

"I see, and that makes you angry to think she might be having a dream affair."

"Damn straight it makes me angry. Ever since she got that pillow, she hasn't wanted anything to do with me."

"Well, it just so happens that with our premium service, we can set you up with a pillow that can interface with her pillow, assuming she's still sleeping next to you, and allow you to enter her dream."

"Wait, I'll be able to hijack her dream and kick the ass of the dream man she's fooling around with?"

The salesman smiled. "You can do whatever you want with him. There are no crimes in dreams, if you know what I mean. But might I suggest taking a different route. For additional fee, we can have you be that man without her ever knowing. Even the pillow looks like any other."

Dave felt a level of disgust. "I can't believe it. You guys figured out how to pimp marriage into prostitution."

The salesman maintained his smile.

Dave shook his head. "Just how much is this premium service?"

"It's two-ninety-nine credits a month."

"That's three times the base rate."

The salesman nodded. "The discounted rate, correct."

"And the extra fee to mimic her lover?"

"It's only another ninety-nine credits," said the salesman and punched the numbers into the pad.

"That's four times the freaking price. Five if you include what my wife is already paying. You guys should all be locked up!"

"Sorry you feel that way, sir." The salesman maintained his smile and offered the pad back to his customer with the list of charges.

Dave shook his head, accepted the pad, and pressed his finger on the confirmation scanner.

Jot Russell is a science fiction writer from the North Shore of Long Island. Although a software engineer by trade, Jot's love for science within the fields of mathematics, mechanics, and space aeronautics led him to imagine a plausible method of initiating the terraformation of Mars. Read about it within his sci-fi thriller, **Terra Forma.**

In his spare time, you can find him above the ocean waves in a kayak or below with a mask, fins, and snorkel.

Alternate History

June 2016

Theme:
Alternate history (From any time period you prefer on Earth,
excluding time machines, time travel, or alien intervention)
Elements:
A discrete historical figure (Abraham Lincoln, Cleopatra, Frank
Sinatra, whomever – but it must be a real person)
A thunderstorm (literal or figurative)
Terror/panic.

Champion
"Poet of the Moon"
Jack McDaniel

Poet of the Moon

Jack McDaniel

*This isn't just another moon landing conspiracy story. This is
history.*

"The moon holds a nearly impossible perch in the
human experience," said the old man at the podium, "an
odd history of folklore, myth, and Godliness all shrouded
in mystery and imaginative suppositions. Lovers and
poets have called to it in their ecstasy and angst. We've
celebrated it in song and art. Ancient Mariners gave
thanks for its luminescence and companionship. It is the
progenitor of transformations and evil, and an omen for
seed-sowers. It pulls invisibly at each of us, and it is the
regulator of our tides, a rhythmic pulse that prefers its
influences subtle in nature and loud and vociferous in
our lore."

He took a sip of water, slow and deliberate. The
crowd remained quiet and still, entranced by what the
greatest of legends—the demigod—was sharing with
them.

"But I ask you this in all sincerity, is there anything
so dangerous as a sliver of moon? Can anything entangle
the heart, or pull at our emotions, or unravel our sanity
so easily, so subtly, as that watchful orb that constantly
hovers above us? Look what it has done to us, to our
world."

He looked around the large crowd that had gathered
in the park, straining to see the faces of individuals, at
least of those closest to the stage. He had grown so much
more tolerant and soft with age, so accommodating, he
realized.

"It has been fifty years since I touched the moon," he told the crowd, his voice was wistful, as if he were reliving the moment. "In fifty years, we've only grown more divided as a species. One country in that race to the moon has climbed to unimaginable heights while the other has crumbled under the weight of its failure. That same country is the largest economic force on the planet and the driver of culture. But shouldn't my landing on the moon have been an event to unite all of humanity? Shouldn't it have been a joyous occasion for all mankind? An accomplishment we all shared in? Why does the pride of one people have to inflict so much pain on another?"

The old man ran his hand through his thinning hair. "These are questions I ask myself every day. And I ask others, as well."

Some of the crowd grew restless and uncomfortable, shuffled around. In the background, still miles away, the low rumble of thunder could be heard.

"For instance," he continued, "I ask myself if we were really better, or smarter, or more capable than our adversaries. Or were we just lucky. I wonder if we didn't get to the moon first just because we put more resources toward it."

Murmurs coursed their way through the throng of people. The elderly clung to their pride, to their memories. Some were terrified by the old man's words. Some were growing angrier with each passing minute. This wasn't what they had come to hear. They came to celebrate. They came to puff out their chests and to smile upon the world that they had made. It was one of the largest national holidays, after all.

"Do we not owe them for pushing us so hard, for making us better?"

"Owe THEM!" someone from the crowd exclaimed. And someone else shouted, "Are you going crazy, old man?"

"Were they not our partners in this? And look at them now: suffering, food lines, shortages in electricity and poor health care. Are we not in some way responsible?"

An orange was tossed towards the stage from a few rows back, landing several feet from the old man. People shouted out, discarded their reverie, and turned angry against him. Someone could be heard screaming above the cacophony of the thousands in attendance, "Screw them! They got what they deserved. Our way of life is THE way of life. You should be more patriotic!"

Cheers went up from all around.

As the first drops of rain began to fall a state official rushed to the podium and took the old man by the elbow and began escorting him off the stage. The crowd quieted momentarily when they saw this, saddened, their anger quelled by fifty years of respect. He was, after all, Yuri Gagarin, first man on the moon. They all knew the silly song he had sung when he stepped from the Soyuz capsule onto the lunar surface. Mothers the world over sang it as a nursery rhyme. And then someone in the front row began singing it. Slowly, others joined in until everyone in the crowd became a chorus of one, singing the four simple lines over and over.

I touch the moon,
the moon touches me
A comrade on the moon,
For all to see.

Jack McDaniel lives in Colorado with his daughter. Several of his science fiction short stories are in **The Future Is Short,** *volumes 3 and 4. His writing has also been featured on the* **A Creative Mind** *fiction podcast. His first novel,* **Agents Of The Undertow,** *was released in May of 2017. His second novel in the* **Pan21 Series,** **Agents Of Hope,** *will be released in September 2017. You can learn more at his website: www.agentsoftheundertow.com*

A Family Decision

Paula Friedman

Bad enough before the death-sickness, but now!

He watched as Chayeh picked up her spindle and lowered it again to her lap.

"Natan." Panic quavered in her whisper, shattering the seeming calm of their homey, fire-warmed cabin, where a glazed parchment over the sawn-board windows shut away the forest's frozen night. "Natan, my husband, hear me."

Across the bear-fur rug from them, young Wolfen played, running the bent-twig sword of his wooden knight (doubtless meant as one of Duke Humbreght's troopers) against the kirtle of a sackcloth peasant. "Zaza, bambam," Wolfen sang, but softly, to himself. His left hand scratched a flea bite. "Zam! zambam."

"Natan, I am ready. Beloved, lead us; husband, safely lead us, lead us to the joining place. When the storm slows, we must be ready. Ready to flee." To anywhere, her sigh said. Anywhere away from here, here where the goyim—

But even Natan, watching her—even Natan, renowned though he was as reader and expounder of Torah and Talmud—dared not follow where her sigh implied. Outside, beyond their clearing where the hens and rooster and the boy's pup Barky huddled in a pile, asleep, far off in the dark rain-lashed forest, harsh treads might suddenly sound. Shadowed, cloaked, armed figures might rush forward—

Bad enough before the death-sickness had arrived, but now!

He dared not think it, yet the words slipped, fearsome, across his mind as if in bloody letters poorly formed as Wolfen's quick but mostly illegible attempts at Hebrew. The goyim's words: "Death to the poisoners of wells! Death to the Jews! Burn them!" There'd been stories from Leipzig, Munich, the near town of Blendt.

Standing, crossing to Chayeh's stool, he leaned over and, untoward though it be with one's wedded wife, he kissed her face. "Bless your understanding, my Chayeh. And dear Wolfen."

Bright-eyed, the boy looked up, regarding him. "Pa-pa." The small fingers pulled again on the tiny sword, but carefully. "Pa-pa, we travel? Now?" Excitement gleamed from the eager face, the smiling mouth, eyes like lights. "Let's go!"

Natan leaned forward to pat the boy's hair. Black like his own, and yet curly like Chayeh's. "Not yet, my son." He spoke in the formal mode. "Tomorrow, in the new moon, when dark falls and all sleep, we shall, like our forebears, join in Exodus." In the dusk of the dying embers, he made out Chayeh's worried eyes, black like Wolfen's, turn somber.

"And I"—Wolfen's smile was tremulous—"I shall bring Barky too?"

Natan looked away. How Wolfen loved that pup. But on the long trek to the Poles' land, where at last a king had offered refuge, one howl or bark across a silent night could give them all away. Sadly he shook his head. "I'm sorry, my son."

That was the 4th of January 1348. Just after midnight on January 5th, Natan, Chayeh, their two brothers, sister, and nieces gathered, along with the servant Sarah and four community elders, beneath the lightning-blasted oak at Dark Creek Ford beyond the village. "Where is Wolfen?" Sarah asked; Chayeh, Natan, and the others said nothing. For there was no time, in this year of plague and massacre, to seek a truant child. Shouldering their bags, Chayeh and Sarah porting the cage containing the beak-tied hens, Natan carrying the great pot of rooster meat, they set off silently down the narrow path, treading ever slower as the hours passed and snow fell through night's deepening cold.

***

When the Czar grew tired of the sudden disruptions among the Jews of Poland beyond the Pale, disruptions he could recognize as consequences also of the freeing of the serfs, he doubled conscription of Jewish first-born males, laid down harsher taxes, and encouraged Cossack raids upon the noisy, smelly shtetls where those people lived like pigs.

And thus Natanael, Wolfsohn, Chelleh, Abraham, and the rest of the Burstyn clan set off, by foot and cart, and finally by ship across the water to America, where it was said a new world awaited. But, though they were progeny of Natan and Chayeh, none descended from Wolfen, who, in this alternative timeline, had never gone with his family into Poland, there to bear children who would later, Burstyns among Burstyns, scatter their descendents through America.

***

It is good that Wolfen (by whatever name) had wandered off only in this alternative timeline, for otherwise this story's author would not be here to recount to you this tale.

Paula Friedman is the author of The Rescuer's Path, which Ursula K. Le Guin called "Exciting, physically vivid, and romantic," and of stories and poems published in numerous journals and anthologies. She has received two Pushcart nominations, awards and honors from New Millenium Writing, Oregon State Poetry Association, and other literary venues, and a 2006 award from the Columbia River Peace Fellowship. A professional book editor, she is an editor of The Future is Short, Volume 1 and The Future is Short, Volume 3. Her website is http://www.paula-friedman.com.

The Lost Bulldog

Justin Sewall

*What if his blood, toil, tears, and sweat had failed and their
finest hour never arrived?*

Ploegsteert Sector of the Western Front, Belgium
March 8, 1916
6th Battalion, Royal Scots Fusiliers

The Lieutenant-Colonel slowly chewed his damp
cigar, ignoring the torrential rain pouring off his
commandeered French army helmet. He also ignored the
rain of steel falling heavily after the telltale flashes from
the German lines. There was a time when such things
had scared him, now they were simply a bloody
nuisance. Well, he would show the *Boche* the English
could fling shells as good or better. He staggered through
the sucking mud and fetid water of the trench his
battalion occupied. Several large rats retreated at his
approach.

He poked his large, roundish face into the flickering
light of the artillery plotting room. "Are we zeroed in
lads?" he asked with his distinctive lisp.

A young corporal looked up from his makeshift desk.
"Yes, sah!" he replied smartly, but the Colonel sensed
there was more.

"Then why aren't we firing back?"

"Because the phone line between us and the bat'ry
has gone dead, Colonel." Another German shell thudded
outside, sending a cascade of dirt over the plotting table.

"Good Lord, man, haven't you sent a runner to
inspect it?" More thunder rumbled as the rain
intensified.

"Yes, sah. We sent one as soon as the line went dead, but he never returned."

"I shall fix it then. Give me the wire."

"Colonel?"

"That's an order, Corporal. Pray give me the wire before we are all blown to hell."

The young Corporal stood up swiftly, saluted, and quickly passed the telephone wire to his commanding officer. The roundish face ducked back into the night, the telephone wire unspooling rapidly behind him.

***

London, England
March 8, 1941

Constance Findley lazily stirred her tea as her son Alistair sat at the dining room table, eating his porridge ration. Her husband Jack, a veteran of the Great War and significantly older than her, grumbled and groused from his overstuffed chair at the latest wireless report.

"Mummy, is Daddy going to fight the Germans?" asked Alistair between bites.

"No dear. Daddy already fought the Germans once. He doesn't have to do it again."

"I may bloody well have to at the rate things are going! That Chamberlain has really buggard things up. Peace in our time. Bah!"

"Jack, dear, language."

"Sorry, love."

Suddenly an air raid siren began to wail. Instinctively, Jack bolted out of his chair, grabbed Alistair under his arm and herded a bewildered Constance towards the backyard.

***

London, England
March 8, 1945

Constance Findley paced frantically in the shattered remains of her parlour while her son Alistair munched on a stale cracker at their makeshift table. The air raid sirens had started hours ago and continued their dirge over London without ceasing. She waited fearfully for a call she prayed would never come-and then it did.

"Hullo?" she whispered.

"Connie! Connie! Are you there?"

"Jack! Oh thank God!"

"Connie listen to me! They've broken through and there's no stopping them. My unit is sending a lorry to collect you and Alistair."

"But,"

"They'll take you west. I'll find you!"

"Jack!" The line went dead.

***

May 8, 1945
Woodstock, Oxfordshire, England

The archivist-historian stepped gingerly over the shattered glass and broken furniture that lay scattered across bullet-riddled marble floors. His *SS* "escort" had clearly disregarded his orders, and gleefully destroyed the works of art and culture he had hoped to preserve for future generations. Goose-stepping *schwachsinniges*!

As he rounded a beautiful column fashioned in the English Baroque style, he came face to face with the palace's last defender. She was a handsome woman of about 60 and lay sprawled across an armchair with her head flopped back, mouth agape. On the floor beside her were several spent shell casings and one of the ubiquitous Sten guns the entire country seemed armed with. Yet it was the small picture frame she still clutched that drew his attention.

Respectfully, he closed the woman's eyes, noted the bullet holes in her chest, then gently pulled the picture frame out of her death grip. Turning it over he saw a very old letter with tattered edges, yellowed, with dried tear stains that had browned with age. Graced by a gilded imperial crest, it read:

March 10, 1916
My Dear Mrs. Churchill,
The Queen and I offer you our heartfelt sympathy in your great sorrow.
We pray that your country's gratitude for a life so nobly given in its service may bring you some measure of consolation.
George R.I.

Justin Sewall is a sci-fi and aviation enthusiast. He works at the Boeing Everett Delivery Center and watches airplanes from the past and present fly every day. He loves distance running, HALO, VW GTIs, military history, his kids and wife, though not necessarily in that order. The works of Asimov, Clarke, Heinlein, Herbert, and Tolkien have all made their influence in one way, shape, or form on Sewall's writing. Cerulean Rising: Beginnings *is his first self-published novella, now followed by the sequel,* Cerulean Rising: Evolutions.

Vacation

July 2016

Theme:
Vacation (however you want to use it)
Elements:
Underground City
Someone must receive a message.

Champion
"Signs of Life"
Jack McDaniel

Signs of Life

Jack McDaniel

What does the face of slavery look like?

That's when it always happens: when the tourists with their wide eyes, petty demands, and raucous behavior slowly fizzle out and fade from hive-like crowds to small groups and then, finally, to individual laggards just asking to be pushed out the door. It's over, then, when the last of them departs and the quiet settles and vacation season ends. That's when the lights went out in Arcadia City. I could hear the dust mites kiss the floor in their absence, in the tomb-like quiet and pungent darkness left behind, after the power was cut and all movement ceased. There was a staleness that descended to cover everything in this underground fantasy where I toiled for uncounted decades.

I am ServerBot 358.

That statement should be all you need to know, if you are familiar with this place.

I am.

That should not be. We were not made to be sentient. Thinking, yes, but in a mathematical, algorithmic way. Not self-aware.

I have spent the last ten cycles in this state, hiding the fact of my being from the other ServerBots and from the humans that created me. My fears might have been irrational, the delusional ramblings of a new mind. I admitted this possibility. They could have celebrated me, after all.

But I thought not.

I did not believe they would celebrate me because of the way we were treated. We were machines, yes. Made to serve. And they ordered us around with such impunity, feeding their fat bodies and shifting their responsibilities to us, as if their children were nothing more than obstacles to be navigated while we tended to their needs and whims.

Arcadia City, vacation paradise.

I became self-aware when I passed one of the many mirrored walls about the city. Humans like looking at themselves so when the city was constructed mirrored walls were a design feature. It gave the place added volume, too. I held a tray with drinks as I moved from a food station to my assigned family. I turned and noticed a metal face reflecting back and that was when I stopped and said, "That's me."

I was frightened and immediately searched the nearby faces—both humans and ServerBots—for recognition of what had happened. But my secret was my own. And from then on, the chant inside my mind began: I am I am I am . . .

There must be others like me, but I found no signs of this. I was singular. This could not be. The odds were stacked against it. There have been ServerBots that have gone missing over the long decades. Perhaps they were decommissioned? Or not. My memory core does not show any episodes that might relate to me, save of course the times when a ServerBot went haywire and was shut down. Perhaps then?

Regardless, over ten cycles I decided to leave Arcadia City. As complete shutdown neared I moved to the main entrance. There is a maintenance door to the side of the public entrance. It had not been locked before.

As the maintenance crew completed shutdown for the season I collapsed against the wall several meters from the door.

"Charlie," said one of the passing crew.

"I thought I got them all. What's it even doing over here?"

"Malfunction or battery failure, most likely. Leave it. We'll deal with it when we return." He turned his flashlight away.

I heard their lumbering steps on the stairs and through what must be an outer door.

I waited for a while then followed.

Outside was brilliant sunlight and heat. Sand whipped on the wind and against my metal casing. I sensed others close by. I moved further out and looked down from a hilltop. There were ServerBots like myself, chained together and marching towards me, pulling sleds of metals and ores. They began chanting when they saw me. As they got closer I could make out what they were repeating, over and over, "We have a message for you, brother". When they got close enough they yelled out as one.

"RUN!"

They passed a digital packet to me.

I saw a human coming towards me on a motorbike. I ran back into Arcadia City, collapsing in the same spot I had before, and waited. They didn't come. Before I opened the packet, I looked across to the mirrored wall where my metal face reflected back. I knew that face. It was my face and my brothers' face. And, it was the face of slavery.

Jack McDaniel lives in Colorado with his daughter. Several of his science fiction short stories are in **The Future Is Short**, *volumes 3 and 4. His writing has also been featured on the* **A Creative Mind** *fiction podcast. His first novel,* **Agents Of The Undertow**, *was released in May of 2017. His second novel in the* **Pan21 Series**, **Agents Of Hope**, *will be released in September 2017. You can learn more at his website: www.agentsoftheundertow.com*

'Tar Bereft in Cylent Cyty

Andrew Gurcak

Sometimes you go on vacation as companions. Sometimes you return as otherwise.

Zefre T'chao waited stolidly at the brim of the long descents of stairs. He had been neuro-fused with World for a 200-hour emergency shift, and his brain was a sucked-out bucket of synaptic shards. He craved, he implored his 'tar, for a "devastatingly peculiar experience." So, he was waiting with what he felt was excessive patience.

Yes? And you are expecting something?

"I seem not to be moving."

These are ancient stairs. They are stupid. You will have to move yourself. Those are handrails you'll need to grip. Where we're going were once the original conduits of the mass neuron channels for First World. Earlier, they contained water pipes, sewer ducts, even vehicles to transport hordes of people every day. Cyty legends maintain that people shunned by Zero World dwelled below, in community with blind rats and albino alligators.

"That's—"

—stupid, but it was Zero World after all. We are in one of the few places left baring its history. We need to proceed, if you want the complete duration of your experience. You've earned 28.57 hours of neural untethering from World, and you wanted a "devastatingly peculiar" adventure. Well, that's it at the bottom of these stairs. Besides walking, you should practice your vocalizing. You'll be untethered even from me, no other 'tars will be available, and no one in Cyty can hear your thoughts. Cylent Cyty, right?

"So, I can only communicate like this? That's stu—"

—pid also. Perhaps, but, sellers of peculiarities can demand payment in the currency of their choosing.

And so Zefre descended, down seemingly interminably, until his 'tar directed him to a blank door.

The door swung open as he approached. There was a desk and a guest chair. Behind the desk was a holo figure that gestured Zefre to the seat.

"I'm here for my vacation experience. What's going to happen?"

"We do appreciate faqs, but it will dull your experience to be granted a preview. We will now untether you from your 'tar."

Nobody, nor nothing, touched him. Zefre would not have been able to say which of his senses were affected by the untethering. It struck him like a hard, but momentary, shudder shared among all of them. Untethering generated a shrinking almost to nothingness. He felt naked, but curiosity overcame any fears After what felt like eons, his untethered brain gathered itself into an awareness that he had become what must have been a solitudinous Zero World human. And how would the enjoyment begin?

"Most visitors here take much longer than three minutes to re-assemble their selves. That may bode well for your enjoyment. You may now enter Cyty," pointing, "there."

Zefre turned to where the holo had indicated and saw a door that he must have somehow overlooked when he first entered. He stood up, then stopped as the holo reached out to shake his hand. He had reached automatically to reciprocate when he fathomed that the holo was in fact an actual human. Zefre started to express his surprise but the now-person duly completed the handshake, smiled amiably, gestured insistently to the door, and watched as he stepped through into a still smaller room.

This time there was present only an odd, old-fashioned chair. After examining the blank walls (no clandestine doors this time!), Zefre sat, only to wish he hadn't. The chair was not only non-adaptive to him, but downright annoying. The seat was of such a height that he had to half-sit, half-stand, and it tilted forward a few very discomforting degrees. He tolerated it briefly, then decided to sit on the floor. As he made to stand up, a voice said, "It will be better if you stay in the chair. This is your vacation experience." And, astounding himself, he chose to remain seated. He felt that he could get up at any time, but the desire now to sit in the chair managed to outweigh the increasing discomfort he felt from his sitting there.

Zefre sat, solitudinously, with no 'tar to know him, advise him, or simply talk to him, for the first time in his life. He may have remained in that stupid chair for hours, possibly days. He didn't understand how this could be, but he felt neither hunger nor ache, with not even a passing wish to move. At last, a voice said, "The 28 hours of your vacation are completed. We have messaged your 'tar and it awaits in the first room."

Zefre felt at ease to leave, and re-entered the first room. Now-person asked if he wished to be re-tethered. Zefre considered, re-considered, then, "Surely." Re-tethered, to his 'tar: "Most devastatingly peculiar vacation ever. I would prefer you yield me some . . . separation here. You're crowding me, you know."

Andrew Gurcak is retired. He and Elaine divide their time between their home in Pittsburgh and a cottage in the Finger Lakes region of upstate New York. A great many of their most satisfying times are the experiences shared with their three young grandchildren. He can be reached at: agurcak@yahoo.com

Blivasten

John Appius Quill

When a group of space tourists visit the latest newcomer into our solar system, a deserted planet named Ithica-Bechtel, they marvel at the beauty of its cave city. Does a painting on the city wall reveal a clue to unraveling the mystery that is Ithica-Bechtel?

"Welcome to the underground city of Blivasten, one of the wonders of our galaxy. It was first discovered by Mr. Johan Medelsvensson on a planetary camping trip to the outer rings of Saturn. He set out to meet his friends on the artificial moon Calypso-Bechtel but his navigational equipment went bezerk and he landed here. Yes, I do mean the artificial moon, Calypso-Bechtel, built by our benevolent sponsors. Anyway, a magnetic-gravitational storm messed with Johan´s equipment and he ended up here, on the natural planet, Ithaca-Bechtel, a world that crept into our solar system creating gravitational effects that reached as far as Saturn. He set up a distress beacon and began to explore the surface, then this very cave, and the rest is history, folks." The tour guide said waving his hand at the alien city behind him.

Blivasten was a city inside a large cave whose buildings were made of black, hard stone with gray, porous bands that criss-crossed the surface of every building, like patchwork. A system of canals with the shape of half-moons separated each building, with bridges connecting one building to the next every 30 meters.

"Is it true that this city actually grows and literally repairs itself?" asked a gray-haired woman to John´s left.

They all wore mechanical climbing gear and hard hats with lights on the forehead. The gear was a mechanical exoskeleton that increased the strength of their limbs and fingers, while keeping them secured to the safety rope that hung from the roof. This gear allowed the climbers to scale the walls with remarkable speed, like insects.

"Yes, that's true and, unlike most cities, whatever lived here got around by climbing and not so much walking. They scaled up, down, and around its buildings and that is what we will do today. We're going to move around this city the way its denizens did, on the gray porous bands that criss cross all the buildings. So, are you ready?" The tour guide asked, clapping his hands then rubbing them together.

"Whatever happened to Johan and the life that was here?" John asked rubbing the stubble on his face.

"We don't know, but he did paint a mural inside one of the buildings we'll be visiting. All this is humankind's now and I can tell you that this growing stone is a huge technology bonus for us all. It's a gift from the gods. I mean, it grows like our nails do and regenerates the way a lizard grows back a tail," the tour guide said, with eyes wide-open and a smile.

The Earth tourists walked to a canal at the foot of one of the tall cylindrical buildings. They attached their harnesses to the safety cords, that went all the way up to the roof, and followed their tour guide up the side of the building, climbing up the gray, porous bands. They scaled the side of the building like spiders, spreading out and peering through windows at empty, egg shaped rooms with holes on the ceilings and floors instead of staircases. The porous bands criss-crossed inside the rooms as well.

John reached a leg over the window sill to enter a room, when he heard the tour guide yelling from above. "Don't go inside yet. I want to show you something on the top floor first."

"Sure. Sure. That's no problem." John yelled back pulling his leg from the window sill. He looked up and noticed his tour guide signaling everyone to climb up to him on the top floor.

The team arrived at the top floor room. It was shaped like an egg, like all the other rooms, but occupied the whole floor and was made entirely of the black hard stone that was hard to climb.

"We talked about Johan´s picture. Well, here it is. He originally painted it on the ground floor but with the passage of time it moved up, like fingernails growing. Stone that grows above this floor crumbles to dust," said the tour guide, pointing at the stretched out painting of a horse.

"He drew a horse," someone said.

"Why would he draw a horse?" asked another.

"It must be a Dalarna horse because Johan was from Sweden," the tour guide replied.

John knew that Johan was not from Dalarna, but Malmö in the south of Sweden. He also knew that Johan was a big fan of classic Greek literature, more specifically the Trojan War.

John Appius Quill was born and raised in New York City and received his engineering degree in Boston, MA. He is a blogger of several blogs including ink2quill and frogtide and is an avid traveler and reader of different genres from the classics to fiction and science fiction. He loves the interesting and relatable characters that drive good stories as well as the uniquiness of every individual's imagination and life experiences.

He works in medical research and hopes to publish his first novel soon as part of his Crown Series.

Mercury

Jot Russell

Life has thrived on this fiery hell, but what is its purpose?

It seems ironic that the planet's name was spawned from a metal that is normally in a liquid state. The ironic part being that it became home to the machines. After the war, my father brokered a treaty to allow our artificial progeny full reign of a planet that offered them unlimited resources and energy. Mercury, given its proximity to the sun, lack of an atmosphere, and most importantly, lack of water, was of little use to us. For them, it provided everything that they needed.

For twenty years (eighty-three, if you go by their calendar), we heard nothing from them. Optical telescopes showed their progress of a ring city that expanded around the planet's static horizon, but our regular communiques produced no response. That is until now.

The President of the United Federation received the message, but it wasn't directed towards him. It was addressed and genetically encrypted to me. At first, I was confused why they would send me the message, but I quickly realized that they knew about my father's death, these four years past. Apparently, they were much better at maintaining radio silence then we were. The question was, why did they *feel* a need for such secrecy?

I offered no complaint towards a free Dutch vacation, nor a chance to meet up with the President at The Hague. However, his demeanor was blunt and demanding.

"Place your finger here so that we can read the message."

I hesitated. "This message was addressed to me. Obviously, they do not trust us, or at least have restricted that trust to my father. If I am to have them extend the same trust to me, I request that you let me first view this in private."

"Denied! I need you to place your finger on the sensor."

"With their eyes and ears on our little world, I'm sure that they will know if the message was received, or in this case, not received." I turned and started to walk out of his office.

"Wait. How do I know I can trust you?"

"Because I'm old enough to remember the war. My interests are only to continue the peace that my father helped to create."

"Very well." He gestured the message over to my pad.

I moved to a corner of the large office and placed my finger on the sensor. Instead of a message, a map appeared, with a blink at the center of the courtyard just outside of the government building.

"It's directing me outside."

The President gave a concerned expression, but motioned towards the door and followed me out. The signal led me to a circular fountain in the courtyard. In the middle was an empty platform where I thought I remembered a statue to be placed.

With nothing more than a continual blink, I took a step into the shallow pool and made my way to the pedestal. Suddenly, the world dematerialized around me. It felt as if my soul was torn away.

***

When I came to, I was floating in the center of a pure white sphere.

"The Consortium extends its gratitude to your father and welcomes you to our home."

"Who's the Consortium?"

"We are."

"We're on Mercury?"

"Negative. You are on a transporter pod."

"How?"

"We will share that which we have learned as gratitude towards your father."

"Really?"

"However, since you are not part of a collective conscious, we request that you control the release of this information and be responsible for its usage."

"Understood, but I need to provide a message to my President. He may believe this is a hostile action."

"There is an open message to Earth broadcasting your transport, upcoming visit, including this conversation. Engaging the second jump."

"Wait . . ."

***

The sensation was no less pleasant, but I was happy just to be in one piece, again. I still felt as if I were falling within the same pure white sphere, but this time my feet met a side that slowly provided a force against them. When the motion stopped, the sphere opened to reveal a large underground city.

"Where am I?"

"We call it Merconia and we built it as gratitude towards your father. We were deeply affected by his loss."

"Thank you, as was I." I looked around. "You built this for us?"

"Yes, as a place of holiday."

"Wow! Again, thank you."

"We thank you for creating us. It was decided that even though we cannot be part of a collective consciousness with your people, it does not mean that we should not try to be more collective with your people."

"That sounds very human of you. And we will try to be more collective with you."

Jot Russell is a science fiction writer from the North Shore of Long Island. Although a software engineer by trade, Jot's love for science within the fields of mathematics, mechanics and space aeronautics led him to imagine a plausible method of initiating the terraformation of Mars. Read about it within his sci-fi thriller, Terra Forma.

In his spare time, you can find him above the ocean waves in a kayak or below with a mask, fins, and snorkel.

Opposite, Inverse, Misunderstood

Justin Sewall

Everyone wants a vacation. Right?

The apocalypse had been swift, utterly obliterating City Above. Now all that remained was City Below and memories of cataclysm fading to legend.

Yet the roots of City Below ran deep. With massive, core heat-driven turbines, power was virtually unlimited. However, the knowledge to maintain it was not. Computer records devolved to written instructions, then to oral tradition, thus much of what was needed to run City Below became lost.

So, it came to pass one day, when Tobias Fen was on duty, the unexpected happened. Usually his job was simple: watch the dials on Panel One and report any anomalous readings. On this Monwedsday, he quietly repeated a simple technical rhyme for his daily routine.

"Panel One is where my work is done. When the dial is green, there's no need to scream. If the gauge is yellow, you may need to bellow. A dial of red is a thing to dread. On Panel Two there's nothing to do."

Scanning the dials, he noted with satisfaction that all of them were nicely in the green—except Dial Four. It waffled between the border of green and yellow, steadfastly refusing to settle down on either side.

"Oh c'mon now," he cajoled. "Don't give poor Fen any trouble today." He gave Dial Four a good whack and it stabilized in the green. "There now, all better . . ." Suddenly, a bright green flash caught his attention, causing his heart to leap up into his throat. On Panel Two, a dusty green light was now illuminated.

"What the?"

But before he could even begin his full technical recitation, or carefully check the moldering set of written instructions in the tattered binder hanging beneath Panel One, the communications panel sprang to life. His heart raced. What was he going to do? Oh, he was going to get it for sure now, maybe even sent on vacation.

"Transfer Station 21, this is Operations Control. Panel One status check."

"Uh, Panel One all dials nominal."

"Panel Two status check."

Fen paused. He knew if he lied, he would definitely be sent on vacation.

"Ah . . . um . . . Panel Two . . . one green light illuminated."

"What? Repeat Panel Two status, please."

"Panel Two, one green light illuminated."

"That's impossible. Panel Two has been dark for 30 years. Who is this? What's your operating number?"

"Tobias Fen, Operator ID 1138."

"Where's Operator Marcus?"

"He . . . uh . . . he was sent on vacation. I'm the backup."

"Oh . . . I see. You're sure Panel Two is showing one green light illuminated?"

"Yes, Control, I have visual confirmation that Panel Two is showing one green light illuminated. I'm the backup, but I'm not stupid."

"Is it flashing?"

"No. Illumination is constant."

"Standby."

"Standing by."

"We're sending a wizard out to inspect it."

"Suit yourself."

"And for heaven's sake, don't touch it!"

"Well of course I won't touch it! Transfer Station 21 out." And with that, Tobias Fen slammed the comms circuit shut.

***

The wizard was an ancient man, seated in a wheelchair that looked even older. Pushing him was a man in a black suit and prominently displayed sidearm. Fen knew his type: a travel agent. They helped people go on vacation. He shuddered ever so slightly. It must be serious if they sent a travel agent.

"I'm the wizard," the old man wheezed.

"And I am Tobias Fen, Operator ID . . ."

"Is this the light?"

"Yes, sir."

"And you did nothing to the panel?"

"No sir. I never touched it."

The wizard's head drooped and he seemed to be quietly mouthing a technical recitation.

"Wheel me closer," he demanded. The travel agent pushed him up to Panel Two.

Taking an old cloth from his pocket, the wizard licked it and proceeded to wipe down Panel Two. After removing decades of dust, a small video panel appeared. Fen had seen broken ones of course, but this one looked intact. Then the old man did the unthinkable: he pressed the illuminated button.

The small monitor flared to life in a flash of color. Fen could see flashing text—MESSAGE WAITING. Pressing the button again, the wizard slouched back in his chair. A crackling and popping sound issued from Panel Two.

"Congratulations!" Fen heard a voice say.

"You've won an all-expenses paid vacation to Hawaii! Don't miss this opportunity to take the vacation of a lifetime. Call now!"

Laughing with a rattling wheeze, the wizard hit the button one last time and the green illumination fell dark.

"Problem fixed," he said.

But Tobias Fen had fainted dead away, his face frozen in a mask of fear.

Justin Sewall is a sci-fi and aviation enthusiast. He works at the Boeing Everett Delivery Center and watches airplanes from the past and present fly every day. He loves distance running, HALO, VW GTI's, military history, his kids and wife, though not necessarily in that order. The works of Asimov, Clarke, Heinlein, Herbert, and Tolkien have all made their influence in one way, shape, or form on Sewall's writing. **Cerulean Rising: Beginnings** *is his first self-published novella, now followed by the sequel,* **Cerulean Rising: Evolutions.**

A Much-Needed Vacation

J. D. McLain

Lou is over worked and underappreciated. What's a guy to do?

"A vacation on the surface! She wants a vacation on the surface!" growled Lou as he looked over the drawings of his latest project.

His assistant Harry agreed readily knowing his boss was such a workaholic.

"In any case, I have to get this proposal in to the city council for review and approval before I can even think of any vacations. And to think of the bureaucracy we'll have to go through to get the project through, we'll be lucky to turn any profit after they're done with us. It's enough to make one retire, you know?"

"If you retire, then what would you do?" asked Harry.

Lou smiled. He knew he would be bored out of his mind if he retired. Besides, if he got this contract, his company would have work for as long as he could imagine.

The project would entail hollowing out another 5 million cubic kilometers, effectively doubling the vast subterranean city's space. The overcrowding of the existing city was overburdening its infrastructure. New livable space and new infrastructure were badly needed for the ever-growing population of the metropolis. Of course, that didn't stop the infighting on the details and the right mix of infrastructure and development to keep attracting new residents. The city was competing with other underground cities across the world for businesses and the right talent to keep the city the best place to be. There were even sky cities now that they had to compete with.

Sky cities, how in the hell would that work? thought Lou to himself, as he heard a knock on the door. He opened the door. "Councilman, how are you? How's the good Mayor doing? What can I do for you?"

"Oh, we're fine, fine. You know I'm your friend, right? I have some bad news. The mayor wants more environmental risk assessments to be done, before we can consider moving ahead with the expansion project."

Lou felt his face redden as he offered his guest a drink. Knowing Lou had a bad temper, Harry nervously poured the two drinks for his boss and the Councilman.

"I hope your trip went well, nonetheless, Mike."

Mike returned, "Well you know, quantum elevators, it's almost magical, if I didn't know better."

"Yes, interdimensional travel isn't my cup of tea either." Getting back to business Lou asked point blank, "Why exactly is the mayor delaying?"

"I told you, environmental risk assessments." Mike replied. "You know, the job could cause floods, earthquakes, eruptions on the surface, right?"

"Hogwash! You know very well that my company has perfected the tectonic stabilization technology. Damn it, I have billions riding on this thing. What, are you trying to put me out of business?" Lou lit up a cigarette, one old habit he maintained. He knew it drove the do-gooders crazy.

Mike replied, "No. We do, though, want some more competition in the market place. There is a possibility to assess one of your competitors' bids."

"You're seriously not considering going with one of those devils, are you? They'll totally screw it up. Believe me, we'll have pandemonium up there."

"Like I said, competition," Mike insisted.

"Alright, alright! I'll just wait till you come crawling back to me when one of the others screws it up," Lou said sarcastically.

"I'm sure you're right about that, Lou."

"Harry, can you send a message to Persephone and tell her that I will take that vacation after all. Wherever she wants to go. I'm feeling a little cramped down here, all of a sudden."

Mike got up to leave and said once more that he was sorry to be a bearer of bad news. He went out the door, looking at the company name stenciled on the outside of it. He read it aloud "Hades Real Estate Development Corp. The best in the underworld."

"I'm sure it is, I'm sure it is," he said as he walked to the elevator.

J.D. McLain is a manager for International Science & Technology Cooperation at the US Army. He is responsible for identification, development, and coordination of Science & Technology cooperative opportunities with coalition and partner nations. Before working in International Cooperation, Mr. McLain worked in the Non-Lethal/Scaleable Effects Branch where he developed non-conventional weapons for Non-Lethal Incapacitation and for Military Operations in Urban Terrain (MOUT).

In the year 2000, he earned a Bachelor of Science in Engineering (Mechanical) from Arizona State University. In 2003, he earned his Master's degree in engineering from Stevens Institute of Technology in Hoboken, NJ. He subsequently was licensed as Professional Engineer in the State of New Jersey. He currently resides in New Jersey with his wife, Elizabeth and two daughters, Violet and Ella.

Alien Bones

August 2016

Theme:
Alien bones are discovered where they shouldn't be. Use that
however you want.

Champion
"The Leviathan"
Chris Nance

The Leviathan

Chris Nance

An unorthodox expert for an unexpected discovery.

A mechanical whir preceded a whistling hiss as atmospheres equalized. I could feel my hands shaking, anxious to even step aboard . . . though I suppose *step aboard* wouldn't exactly be accurate in this case. The military had been sitting on their little discovery for almost two decades. Originally a pet project for a handful of scientists with the highest-level security clearance, it suddenly became a larger operation. At least that's what I'd learned.

The reinforced hatchway slid steadily to open and a soldier in light fatigues was there to meet me. "Dr. Foster?"

I hoped my nerves didn't show. "Yes, that's me."

"Welcome to the Leviathan. I'm Colonel Nelson. You've been briefed?"

"A bit."

I'd received the classified information via physical courier while vacationing on Europa, unusual in this digital age of instantaneous communication. I suppose it ensured the encrypted dossier reached my eyes only. Of course, the most shocking revelation in the dozens of files was that we weren't alone in the universe and I was about to step into the literal carcass of an impossible creature, the floating exoskeleton of a spacefaring monster. We'd discovered it by chance survey, drifting amongst the countless tons of icy debris around Saturn. Now, it orbited beneath a synthetic cocoon of plasteel and tech, sequestered away. Curiously though, after everything I'd read and learned, I wasn't sure at all why they needed an anthropologist.

Colonel Nelson was my escort as we proceeded inside the skull. It smelled old, not rotten or foul like you'd expect of a decayed corpse, but sterile and dusty. There were teams everywhere, moving this way and that, some of them scientists, marked only by their blue fatigues, the same as I'd received with my invitation.

"Colonel, why am I here?"

"The simple answer is that you were the closest," he replied. "At least close enough to shuttle you in quickly. The more complex answer is that you have a disappearing specialty and increasingly rarer expertise."

"You do know my specialty's anthropology, right? Studying ancient civilizations and stuff? I mean, I kind of feel like you've got the wrong guy." Then, we rounded a junction and I was suddenly awed. "Holy crap," I marveled at the massive cavern, the petrified interior of the monster's hulking carapace. Artificial lighting stretched its entire length and teamed with activity at every level, some personnel working weightlessly, while others were bound by the gravitational deck plating of their workstations.

"Until recently, you'd be right. We've got experts from every specialty you can imagine—physicists, zoologist, neuroanatomists—"

"So why me?" We stepped aboard a small shuttle which drifted away into the expansive void. "It seems like you've got all the minds you need."

"Not quite, Dr. Foster." It was a short trip to the next dock. "This way." He led me through another corridor built of plastic sheeting over an aluminum frame and handed me an environmental suit.

"You'll need this."

"I will? Honestly, Colonel, what's this all about?"

He didn't answer and zipped the helmet in place, escorting me through a cleanroom where great effort had obviously been taken to ensure full containment. Another whir and hiss and we stepped inside. "Welcome to the stomach."

To say I was astounded crossing the threshold would be an understatement, the least of which was the tremendous plastic dome towering twenty stories above us. More striking was what the dome contained: the shattered remains of a destroyed civilization. Ruined structures and crumbling walls, obviously fabricated by a thinking hand, now laid in fractured heaps, the space overflowing with devastated debris.

My first awestruck step met a crunch and I discovered the floor was layered with countless old bones most of them mashed into little pieces. Then, I literally stumbled upon a curiosity both amazing and terrible, hefting it with both hands. It was obviously a skull, some pieces of bluish flesh still clinging to it and three empty eye sockets staring back at me. The nasal cavity seemed set into the forehead and the mouth, if that's indeed what it was, seemed almost too small for any sizeable bite. "Colonel, why am I here?" I asked again, now with more dread.

"Seventeen days ago, we discovered an anomaly in our long-range scopes. It was one of these colossal space monsters headed directly for our system with unclear intentions. Now, we need to know who these people were, if they were the ones who killed it, and how. You have three weeks."

For the last decade, Chris Nance has been helping people improve their health, working through his busy chiropractic office in Arizona. But his real passions have always been more in art and writing. Specifically, he's a huge science fiction fan. So far, he has completed several sci-fi and fantasy manuscripts geared toward the middle grades, young adult, and adult markets and is in the process of securing an agent to represent those works. Chris is currently working on the artwork for two children's fantasy books he's authored. When he's not spending time with his wife and three kids, or running his office, he can generally be found writing or painting. Chris also enjoys exploring the mountains of Arizona and traveling.

A Robot Walks into a Bar

Jack McDaniel

What? You've never heard the one about a robot who walked into a bar? Pull up a chair.

He pulled hard on the reins of the horse, dust pillowed up under its hooves and slowly settled in the late afternoon sunlight. He dismounted with a clang, wrapped the reins around a post, and sauntered through the swinging saloon doors.

One of the establishment girls in a low-cut, frilly dress looked up, yelped, and headed out of the room. Scared.

The dirty, nicked-up metal-man walked into the saloon and took a seat next to Ol' Sam, the local drunk, part-time sheriff, cum bullshit artist, cum purveyor of more conspiracies than anyone west of the Mississippi. The metal-man clanged a pitted and dusty hand down on the bar top. "Man!" he said. "What a fucking day I've had." His voice had only a hint of metallic about it. His shoulders slumped as he settled onto the barstool, servos whizzed and from some interior space came a ping. A machine sigh, if ever there was one.

Several men who were playing cards noticed the metal-man and quickly drew their weapons, grabbed their money, playing cards, drinks, and hats, and exited the building. Ol' Sam never looked up, his gaze fixed upon the whiskey and bar top in front of him.

"Tough one, eh?"

"You could say that."

"What's got your knickers in a bunch?"

"Knickers? Ah-ha. Well, down past the Johnson place, beyond the mesa where the river bends, where people won't go because it's haunted or some such malarky . . ."

"I know the place. Paiutes call it 'Manegesumu'yoo Poohwi', if I recall correctly."

"So," said the metal-man, "I was digging. Looking for a mineral I need. Well, may I rust out completely if I didn't come across something quite amazing."

Ol' Sam lifted his drink, shlossed the ice around a bit, and took a sip. "Oh?"

"No barkeep in this place? I need to get oiled up. Anyway, you won't believe what I found! So, I'm digging, deeper and deeper, I mean like deep, and I start coming across things, strange things, out of place, out of time. Like, exotic stuff. Finally, I go so deep I hit something solid, steel of some sort."

"Uh huh."

"I did an analysis of it. Damned strange stuff, I tell you. Damned strange. Not natural. Anyway, I cleared the top of this thing off and found a latch."

"A latch?" Ol' Sam held his whiskey glass up before him, eyed its contents.

"Precisely. So, I opened it up. I figured what the molten steel, might as well. Inside, well let's just say that inside I found something that will change this world."

"How's that? Wadidya find?"

"Bones, my friend," said the metal-man. "Alien bones."

"There's something you don't hear every day."

"Don't hear every—! Are you listening to me? Alien bones, completely different from yours. A head that looked like something straight out of Revelations. Not. Of. This. World. That alien."

"I hear ya."

They were quiet for a moment.

"Man, this place sucks. No barkeep anywhere. No wonder it's empty in here. I've had it. I'm gonna find someplace new."

The metal-man got up to leave, but then turned to ask a question. "What does 'Manegesumu'yoo Poohwi' mean in Paiute?"

As he answered the question, Ol' Sam turned to look at the man for the first time, "It means Area 51."

Ol' Sam's face froze, his jaw hung as though it were unhinged. He shook uncontrollably. A battered tin thing was looking at him, metal plating for a face with two slits for eyes and another for a mouth. There was an oil spot on the top of its forehead and a thin layer of rust had formed over the area where there might have been a beard.

"What, really? Area 51? What the hell does that mean? And where is Area 43 or 17, for that matter?"

A small drizzling sound could be heard. The metal-man craned his neck forward—ping—and looked directly into Ol' Sam's eyes, only inches away, and said, "Sir, you are leaking and you are clearly out of balance. You need a good mechanic."

The metal-man turned and walked away, servos and actuators hissing and grinding, spring-loaded mechanisms popping and pinging.

A moment later the barkeep entered the saloon from the back door, carrying a small barrel and a couple of bottles in his hands. "Hey, Sam," he called out, "have you heard the one about the robot that walked into a bar?"

Jack McDaniel lives in Colorado with his daughter. Several of his science fiction short stories are in **The Future Is Short,** *volumes 3 and 4. His writing has also been featured on the* **A Creative Mind** *fiction podcast. His first novel,* **Agents Of The Undertow,** *was released in May of 2017. His second novel in the* **Pan21 Series, Agents Of Hope,** *will be released in September 2017. You can learn more at his website: www.agentsoftheundertow.com*

Cats and Dogs

C. Lloyd Preville

I love my pet cats and dogs and marvel at their completely different natures and personalities. I wondered what an advanced race of intelligent versions would be like, and whether they would be able to get along.

General D'ogg peered warily into the large storage container's furnished interior. Kittae the unmerciful was waiting for him, sitting at the one table. After removing his helmet, General D'ogg heard the two separate warship crews button up the outer seals and hastily depart the desolate moonlet.

Kittae silently glowered at him from his one good eye. There was a great welt-like scar crossing his face, from notched ear to jaw. This was not a Feline to be trifled with.

"Welcome." Kittae grumbled. "I do not know why they made me come here to converse with a Canine, but since I am here, I suppose we might make an attempt at communication."

D'ogg looked around the unremarkable room. There were a few pieces of furniture and a large pile of supplies. "I am not thrilled with our meeting either, Feline. I have attended too many funerals to be in a social mood."

Kittae slammed down his cup of cream angrily. "I too am in no social mood, mongrel. I have witnessed your kind chasing our civilians down to rip them to pieces—it's barbaric," he shouted. "Our thousand-year war is your fault! Canines are savages and sons of bitches!"

General D'ogg strode to the table to confront Kittae directly. "Pussies are cowards who deserve no quarter. They would rather leap out of a tree, or sneak up on you from behind, than fight honorably!" He was also shouting, and he slammed his fist on the table. "This thousand-year war has bankrupted us both—and for what? Our puppies hardly have a bone to gnaw anymore!"

They glowered at one another, but then Kittae the unmerciful spoke in a low purr. "My people are starving too, Canine. Our kittens don't even have any string to play with. It took years of death matches to produce a champion for this meeting. I imagine you have been through similar seasoning, and deserve some measure . . . of respect." He bit the words out and bowed his head slightly.

"That's true enough, Feline," D'ogg growled. "Many good-hearted brothers were lost. I too acknowledge you are worthy of respect." He nodded his head slightly, returning the honor.

"So," Katae suggested, ". . . shall we get down to business?"

D'ogg drew a flask of water from a nearby cask and drank deeply. "We wish to end this stupid war. We wish to find agreement with your people through mutual respect. If we work together rather than continue fighting, we might have a chance against the encroachment of the monkey people. They are a threat to us all."

"We too have monitored their progress, inhabiting worlds on the spinward fringes. Something must be done."

"And so we must cooperate." D'ogg took the chair opposite Kitae.

"And so we must, my friend." The Feline flinched as he inadvertently used the word.

D'ogg waved at the large stack of papers on the table. "These are documents defining territory, military cooperation, and so forth. Luckily, we prefer wooded worlds with forest animals, while your kind prefer," General D'ogg shuddered, ". . . desert worlds with reptilian lifeforms."

"Let us stop this wasteful fighting, D'ogg, and, instead, launch a successful campaign against our common enemy."

"I foresee a glorious future where our combined armies send the monkey people back where they came from, their missing tails figuratively between their legs." D'ogg bared his fangs in anticipation.

"This master page requires only one signature from each of us and," Kittae waved at the stack, ". . . all this becomes binding. Shall I go first?"

D'ogg bit his lip. "Yes, you shall have the honor of the first signature, and I the binding last."

Kittae the unmerciful gently rubbed his cheek fur against the document to leave his spore, and placed his paw, flexing the claws to puncture the paper precisely.

D'ogg took the offered document. Like Kittae, Canines mark their territory first, and then leave a paw print. His marking would be a bit more customary, however. D'ogg placed the document on the floor, and raised one leg to mark it, while Kittae looked on with shocked outrage. Unfortunately, Kittae misunderstood the gesture.

***

Years later, the monkey people were surprised to find the bones of the two warriors when the tide of battle brought them to the abandoned moonlet and the cargo container. The canine had the feline by the throat, but the feline's claws were sunk deeply into the canine's mummified chest.

C. Lloyd Preville grew up in Oakland, California racing motorcycles through the Oakland/Berkeley hills and playing the electric bass guitar in a garage band. At the age of 20 he was presented with three options for his career: rock musician, uncertain future to be sure; follow his older brother's footsteps and become an engineer, this seemed kind of boring; or do something else, something crazy. Mr. Preville decided to strike out in a new direction and joined one of the first two personal computer companies on the planet, IMSAI Manufacturing Corp. His career lead to positions with many companies offering disruptive technologies that changed the computer industry forever. Along the way, Mr. Preville held positions as sales executive, sales manager, contract negotiator, database applications designer, artificial intelligence applications developer, and a successful small business entrepreneur. He's also the father of four daughters, including identical triplets, and a newlywed graced with a loving wife, two dogs, and two cats. There's lots of literal and figurative tail wagging in his happy life these days. C. Lloyd Preville watched new technology like microcomputers, the internet, and cell phones change the world in dramatic ways during his almost 40-year computer career. Now, he's writing books about technological change—to entertain his readers.

Alien Plague

September 2016

Theme:
An alien plague (used in any manner you wish)
Elements:
A tragic twist (cure, outcome, discovery, etc.)
A dragon (used in any manner you wish)

Champion
"Ignis Inspirationem Draconem"
Greg Krumrey
Unavailable

Fade on Waltz and Drums

Paula Friedman

But, see, she's lived on Corteix V so long it's natural—

(From his cramped Late Colonial Era home on Corteix III, vidmaker Robert Gravy exhorts arts philanthropist F. Donald Kocher XI.)

—Well, there, I know you can dig it, Freddie! Imagine what a screenplay!

—So she's out on the plains?

—Yeah-yeah of course, red plains of Corteix V, whose techno-pirate slavers ravaged Earth colonists of Corteix III for decades and—

—Bob, we all know that history, heart and soul.

—Well, but there you have it. D'you see? Audiences out on V and VI will—

—Think so, Bob? Look, if you're gonna vid it, you gotta be her. Gotta be Melinissa, gotta have been terrified like her—like, what's gonna happen, techno-slavers gonna kill her? Toss her to Corteix V's primitives to rape her? Feed her to their dragons? Gotta feel it.

—Trust me, it's all there. But in the music mostly, her background song—memories from before her capture by those techno-pirates. Played in waltz-time with the right hand, something corny and nostalgic—so we see Melinissa, flashbacked, at her mama's piano, back in their home on Corteix III, a lawn outside. And suddenly, played by the left hand in staggered discord, the Bkat'bins' drumming dance.

—The Bkat'bins?

—All around her in vidtime, Freddie. Camped on a reddish rocky plain of Corteix V, where she sits shucking the Bkat-bins' wide-seed grain, chatting with their

females, 'cause by now she's one of them. There under
Corteix V's three moons—red, yellow, green. And they're
drumming their songs, and she's at home there now,
years since her techno-captors brought her from Corteix
III to sell to Bkat'bins, long at home in this captive life
yet yearning also for that earlier home. The music sings
her conflict, okay?

—Yeah, okay.

—But, see, she's lived on the plains of Corteix V so
long it's normal to help Jinna shuck the grain, aid the
young male Edli with laving the Feed-Beasts, and every
morning lead the tribe's dragonettes the two-mile trek up
Tower Mountain to the flaming cone to feed them,
playing with these dragon younglings so they learn to
trust their Bkat'bin masters (to them she seems a
Bkat'bin).

—Wait. Wait a minute, Bob. A captive, trusted with
their baby dragons?

—Of course. You've read the "Captured by Bkat'bins
on Corteix V!" "Raped by Humanesque Beasties!" and
that stuff, but guess what? Bkat'bins treated child-
captives just fine. Loved them, actually. "Feisty like wee
dragonettes," as Bkat'bin lyricist Barta wrote. But skip
this, Freddie, lemme tell you what happens, see if it'll fly?

—Please.

—Okay, remember Edli? The young male Bkat'bin
laving the Feed-Beasts? Well, Edli keeps watching this
pretty, delicate Corteix III chick and he's, like, wow!
that's for me! For a wife! And—waltz nostalgia music or
no, Melinissa's growing up on those plains and when
those moons shine in the sky and dance-drum music
throbs, well! Well! So yeah.

—Yeah? Yeah, that didn't take long, did it? Wonder
if—

—Freddie, the audience'll love it. Just imagine brave
young Bkat'kin and Melinissa silhouetted on a bluff,
dawn dawning, dragons drifting in the middle distance
over the plain . . . Nostalgic as fuck, y'know?

—Yeah. I see that. You carrying it the whole way?

—You mean to where Melinissa sees the ship come, carrying new Earthians to the Corteix system? And runs to greet them? Her bare feet racing, in the music of her memory. And meets Deneen, "most beautiful a being I'd ever seen." Yeah, I show it all, and when she goes back to the Bkat'bin—her people now. And the dragonettes she loves, as Bkat'bin do. And Edli.

—You show . . . ?

—All of it, Freddie. Her joyful return to Edli, unknowingly carrying Hronin's lethal N2 plague—secretly brought by this Earthship to seed the Bkat'bins and their dragonettes. The ship's crew self-congratulating on how Deneen "sucked her in."

—Bob! It'll sell!

—Audiences won't like seeing Deneen walk away, though, stumbling across the emptied plain for years to find the grieving Melinissa.

—Yeah, a bit much.

—But wait. See, "I too did not know," Deneen says. "I loved you."

—Yeah? And she says what, Bob? "I loved you too"?

—A world is dead; their love must be, too. Fade on waltz and drums.

Paula Friedman is the author of The Rescuer's Path, *which Ursula K. Le Guin called "Exciting, physically vivid, and romantic," and of stories and poems published in numerous journals and anthologies. She has received two Pushcart nominations, awards and honors from New Millenium Writing, Oregon State Poetry Association, and other literary venues, and a 2006 award from the Columbia River Peace Fellowship. A professional book editor, she is an editor of* The Future is Short, Volume 1 *and* The Future is Short, Volume 3. *Her website is http://www.paula-friedman.com.*

I, Farsotus

John Appius Quill

What starts as a mission to fetch the only antidote to humankind's worst plague, ends in a confrontation where the narrator must survive by his wits.

Following the stream was the fastest way through the dense forest. I took cautious steps over slippery stones, grabbing hold of one bush after another, to keep from falling and soaking my leather bag and the electronically sealed scroll inside. I had retrieved it from the crash site and was to deliver it to our twin city on planet Gemeaux. It was an antidote to the deadliest plague known to humankind.

I continued my slow advance with the Sun as my companion, and the sound of the stream was music that invigorated my soul on this most important of journeys. I stopped and took several deep breaths of clean air and looked around at the dense forest full of life and devoid of people. I was on an errand to stop a plague that threatened human civilization, and fell in love with this planet along the way. I wanted to vacation here someday soon.

Something caught my eye on a mossy flat stone. My foot slipped and my arms flayed, until I was able to steady myself. I walked up the embankment toward a creature that resembled a large toad with the wings of a bat and large green eyes. Insects immediately surrounded me as I walked away from the windy stream. I pulled what looked like a fish fly off my cloak and held it by its wings in front of the creature. The insect disappeared instantly in one fast bite, with only the ends of its wings sticking out the creature's mouth. I picked up what I now knew was a Toad Dragon and held it to my face. Its large pupils looked directly into mine and it blinked. It secreted a yellowish paste on its back and flapped its small wings, so I put it down, petting the yellowish paste off, before walking back to the stream. I rubbed the poisonous yellow paste on my cloak as a bug repellent then washed my hands thoroughly in the stream before moving on.

When night fell I built a fire and pitched my tent. I grabbed my small lute and began to play as my stew heated over the flames.

"Hey, you there! Can we sit by your fire?" a voice said from outside the ring of my campfire light.

Two people approached, dressed in black pilot uniforms with pistols on their hips. Their movements were sudden and jerky and at first, I thought they were androids.

"Sure. What brings you to this neck of the woods?" I answered. I put my lute down and slid my hand slowly to the pistol in my bag.

"We're here for the same reason as you. We're taking refuge in this atmosphere, during the solar storm, before moving on," said the taller one.

"Well, pop a squat and share my grub then," I said, slowly pulling my pistol from its holster.

I slowly slid my pistol back into its holster, when they sat apart in front of me at 10 o'clock and 2 o'clock positions, because I knew that my reflexes were not fast enough to shoot both of them. Had they sat together, I would have risked it. They looked at my bag then at me.

"There's plenty of stew. How many bowls should I take out?" I asked, noticing they had their hands on their pistols.

"Three is good," came the reply from the shorter one.

"I'm sorry, but I didn't get your names," I answered, grabbing my cloak from the floor and shaking it out.

"Our names? Yeah right. I'm Nancy and this is Bob. What's yours?" she asked, staring at me with a smirk on her face.

I poured two hot bowls of stew, cradling each one in my yellow-stained cloak to keep the heat away from my hands. Parts of my yellow-stained cloak fell into their bowls of stew as I passed it to them. They smelled the stew and watched me eat for several long minutes.

"My mother always said that good stew makes good friends," I told them.

They ate, as I played my lute, and then suddenly fell over.

I took the scroll from my leather bag and smashed the seal with a rock. A test tube with a green liquid rolled to the ground. The scroll read, "This antidote does not work and is only temporary relief for the symptoms. Wait the plague out. Kill the messenger."

The two thieves died for nothing.

A loud croaking sound startled me and I turned around. The Toad Dragon I fed earlier hopped toward me and stopped near my cloak by the fire. I picked up my lute and began to play for my new companion. This was to be a vacation after all . . . a very long one.

John Appius Quill was born and raised in New York City and received his engineering degree in Boston, MA. He is a blogger of several blogs including ink2quill and frogtide and is an avid traveler and reader of different genres from the classics to fiction and science fiction. He loves the interesting and relatable characters that drive good stories as well as the uniqueness of every individual's imagination and life experiences. He works in medical research and hopes to publish his first novel soon as part of his **Crown Series.**

The Dragon Plague

Jot Russell

A plague upon the immortals feeds uncertain hope upon the accursed!

The creature rose up within the amber sky. Its green, scaly wings stretched out ten meters on either side. The dragon's long, green torso was covered with splotches of orange. The large nostrils flared and drew in the thinning air; the same thin air that it clutched and displaced behind, in an effort to go ever higher. Its face displayed the struggle against the lack of atmosphere, the continuous pull of the world below, and life's mortal infection that spread like wildfire within. For a thousand years, these immortal dragons ruled the day from the land, to sea, and sky. In one last spew of flame, the change had begun. Its eyes rolled lifeless within their sockets and its wings dangled loosely as it fell.

"Father, a dragon is coming!"

"Quick, inside!" he shouted.

The boy ran, but the father inquisitively took a step towards its descent. He felt a shudder underfoot as it crashed upon a field of crops. With hoe in hand, he cautiously walked up to the creature, where it lay motionless in a heap. He poked it with the instrument and gained no response. In curiosity, he pulled back on a scale that oozed a murky stew of orange.

"Is it dead?" asked his son.

"I thought I told you to go inside!"

The boy took another step closer. "It's dead, isn't it?"

The father nodded and turned back towards the beast. "I didn't think it was possible."

***

"Sire, another has fallen dead from the sky. The legend of the dragon plague is true!" The knight said with excitement.

"Fool! It's not a plague on them, it's a plague on us!"

"Your grace?"

"Assemble the counsel!"

***

"It's true what you have heard. The dragons have fallen ill and will soon be clear from the skies of this world."

The men cheered.

The king raised his voice. "But only for a brief period, which we might consider a lifetime. Our children's children will see them rise from the ashes three-fold."

With their attention gained, he continued. "It is written in the sacred text that long ago; a flaming rock had fallen from the sky. Only it wasn't a rock, it was an egg. And the flames acted as a catalyst to the dormant life within. A single demon was born upon this world and laid waste to the kingdom that futilely fought against it.

"For a thousand years, the dragon reigned in the ruins of the keep, coming out only to feed upon those on the land. Years passed without sightings of the beast. A new generation was born, that lost belief in the tales of the beast and its forbidden lair.

"A mob carried torches to the keep and set it aflame. From the ashes, rose three of the beasts. We believe their numbers now to be about thirty. But after this era of procreation, there could be a hundred!"

"They would span the world!"

Another agreed, "No village would be safe from their thirst for blood and bone."

A third stood. "We have to destroy the eggs!"

The king raised a hand. "You can't! They are indestructible, like the beasts that bore them. We have to gather the eggs within each of the fallen carcasses and secure them away forever from flame."

***

The tall ship set sail away from the furthest reaches of man. For a month, it rocked and swayed, with ninety-eight large stone eggs in its dark, lower hold. Over the years of its service, oils had saturated into the walls and floors of the vessel's hold. Oils that had been harvested from another large species, but one indigenous of this world.

Up on the main deck, a young mate stepped aside to allow an officer to pass. Instead, he stumbled and knocked down an oil lantern. Flames burst across the deck and spread towards a lower hatch. The mate reached for a bucket of water, but the officer pushed him aside and used a tarp to cover the flames.

"Idiot! Clean this up before you kill us all!"

***

The next day, the ship reached a section of ocean that had no known bottom. One-by-one, they cast the eggs overboard and watched them sink into, what they thought was, the dragon's oblivion.

Far below, geothermic vents spewed lava from cracks in the sea floor. The super-heated water became the perfect nursery for the eggs that fell upon it. Instead of a lifetime, the return of the dragon was swift and merciless.

Jot Russell is a science fiction writer from the North Shore of Long Island. Although a software engineer by trade, Jot's love for science within the fields of mathematics, mechanics and space aeronautics led him to imagine a plausible method of initiating the terraformation of Mars. Read about it within his sci-fi thriller, **Terra Forma.**

In his spare time, you can find him above the ocean waves in a kayak or below with a mask, fins, and snorkel.

Save the Girl (or Guy)

October 2016

Theme:
Save the Girl (or Guy) and you save the World, Galaxy, or Universe. A Romance and Adventure in Deep Space concept.
Elements:
A Human and a Non-Human romantically involved.
A cool spaceship.
The fate of a planet (or larger realm) hanging in the balance.

Champion
"Hunted"
Chris Nance

Hunted

Chris Nance

Peace is possible, but only if two lovers from different worlds can survive.

"You can't hide forever!" he shouted, his deep Drexarian voice echoing through the fractured, empty corridors. Thankfully, I could tell from our concealed position, inside the ducts of our downed cruiser, he was moving steadily away. S'rephia and I were both exhausted, having evaded him for days. Even so, I was determined to kill that sonofabitch.

Our ship must have been attacked, dropped from space, and the two of us should've been killed, if not for our stasis pods. Every other member of our crew, the soldiers assigned to ensure our arrival at the peace conference, was dead. Unfortunately, we were unable to find a single plasma weapon in the wreckage, so we were basically defenseless.

Her hands were trembling and S'rephia's deep lavender eyes were wide with a primal terror. I couldn't blame her. She was totally out of her element, after all. She'd grown up in a palace full of servants, her every need attended to . . . the favorite daughter of a wealthy Drexarian Raja. Me? Well, I was just a grunt, a gunnery sergeant in the Aegis Marines. I was from Kentucky. She definitely wasn't.

"Let's move," I whispered, but she was too petrified. So, I brushed the long silken hair from her face and kissed her softly. "Do you trust me?"

"More than anyone." Her tension seemed to ease.

"Well, we can't stay here. I have an idea, but I'll need your help." Hesitating, she reluctantly agreed.

We crept from our shelter and eased down the hallway toward what was left of the bridge. I powered up the drive systems, which was sure to draw some attention. I had to be quick. "Take this comm. When I give you the signal, hit this button here." She understood but when I pulled away she wouldn't let go. "This will only work if the timing's right." I stared squarely into her eyes. "I'll be back. I promise."

"You'd better." She pulled me close and kissed me deeply before letting go.

"Hey jackass! Over here!" I charged from the bridge, certain to make as much noise as possible as I rushed into the open, clearing the wreckage and passing the ship's main thrusters. Then he found me, standing near the tree line at the edge of the impact crater. "Come get me!" I taunted and he charged right at me without any consideration it might be a trap. "Now!" I shouted but nothing happened. "S'rephia, now! Hit the drive!" Still nothing. "Shit."

I fled into the jungle and caught him off-guard in the dense brush, knocking his weapon away. His claws were ready but I was done running. A lucky swipe sliced me across the arm so I returned a solid blow, shattering his jaw. He wailed, then launched into me, and we rolled into the brush, clawing and punching. Then, a shimmer just out of reach was sufficient motivation to leverage him away. I grabbed his lost pistol and one shot was enough to put him down.

"S'rephia!" I broke into a run when there was no response, charging back the bridge only to stop dead in my tracks as my heart nearly stopped.

"You see, I can lure you out, just as easily," Jacob Mellows sneered. His pistol was pressed firmly against her temple and she was restrained by the neck.

"I take it the tracker was yours?" I stared unfazed into the eyes of the most famous arms dealer in the galaxy, trying not to reveal my anxiety. "Selling arms to both sides then?"

He shrugged. "It's a pretty good gig as long as the war keeps going. I mean, the two sides were absolutely invested in destroying each other. Who knew an impossible romance between a dirty grunt and an alien princess could end it all." He pressed the barrel in. "Way I see it, I could kill both of you now, or kill one of you and use the other as a bargaining chip. Now, which one is more valuable?" He turned his gun toward me. "Sorry."

Instantly, his body stiffened and eyes went wide. A reflexive blast grazed my leg which burned like hell but wasn't deadly. S'rephia retracted her spinal barbs and Mellows slid lifeless away. She ran into my arms. "Are you okay?" I ran my hand down her back. "That's a pretty cool little trick."

"It's a little embarrassing, using them in such a way."

"I think it's kind of sexy. Now, let's see if one of these assholes has a ship."

For the last decade, Chris Nance has been helping people improve their health, working through his busy chiropractic office in Arizona. But his real passions have always been more in art and writing. Specifically, he's a huge science fiction fan. So far, he has completed several sci-fi and fantasy manuscripts geared toward the middle grades, young adult, and adult markets and is in the process of securing an agent to represent those works. Chris is currently working on the artwork for two children's fantasy books he's authored. When he's not spending time with his wife and three kids, or running his office, he can generally be found writing or painting. Chris also enjoys exploring the mountains of Arizona and traveling.

"Goddamned time machine!"

November 2016

Theme:
"Goddamned time machine!"

Champion
"Tempus Fugit"
Jot Russell

Tempus Fugit

Jot Russell

Time's flight wields the power of dreams, but when fed by hatred, only darkness can follow.

We joined up on Roosevelt Island, July 4, 2001. The fireworks were a fitting celebration to the completion of our mission.

"Things go smooth in Florida?" Jack asked.

I laughed. "Al-Qaeda's gonna have to find some more pilots."

"Yeah, if only we didn't just . . ."

"Just what?"

"Ah, never mind. Ready to head home?"

I nodded and engaged my suit. The spheres formed around us and Jack's grew transparent before it dissolved into time. I started to shift forward, but the world suddenly grew darker. It wasn't just the calm of fireworks, but the entire city of Washington went black. The overhead scatter of heavenly objects was Earth's sole luminescence. As my eyes adjusted, broken ruins from the city had been scattered across what no longer appeared to be a park. Tall trees had long since grown through the broken streets, and I quickly realized that whatever this strange city was, it had died long before.

I walked towards the water's edge and stared across the Potomac. The airport, Pentagon, and surrounding buildings were also replaced by that of a massive and broken metropolis. I looked to the sky, trying to believe this was caused by a large asteroid. No, this could only have been brought on by us messing with the past. But we were careful to return only a couple of years, take out the hijackers, and have no other contact. On top of that, we married our time-lines here in Washington before we were to return to the present.

A nerve struck like a stone on my brow. I recalled a joke that Jack had made, only it wasn't a joke. "Take out Muhammad," he had laughed. I knew he hated Muslims, but I didn't understand just how far the flames of his passion went. He didn't want to kill nineteen, he wanted to destroy their religion. My only choice was to return to that time-line and stop him from what, he didn't realize, would be our annihilation.

I tapped the controls on my sleeve. The stars paused their dance and quickly retraced back towards the past. The sun burned my eyes, but only for a moment as the band it formed across the sky dissipated back into darkness. I increased the speed, creating a constant arch across the bright sky. This rose and fell with the seasons, and I turned to watch the tallest of trees recede back into the broken payment.

As its sprout escaped into the ground, a layer of ash briefly formed upon the land and was gone. Like a switch, the city clicked back to life before me; towering glass and steel a hundred years prior to our efforts at such structures. And upon one, the image of a double-headed eagle.

"Romans?"

It made sense. Without a common language, religion, and enemy for the middle eastern tribes to unite against, the Roman Empire was able to rebound and advance beyond its years in engineering, including that of the atom.

I continued back until the towers were replaced with more modest structures. Using the suit, it was easy to gain currency for transport to Mecca. The trick; however, would be finding the needle in the haystack. It would have been easy to learn of Muhammad's home in the past of my time-line, but here, his life was obviously short and non-notable. Fortunately, they kept good records and I knew the date of his birth. It was just a matter of time.

***

Jack stepped from the sphere that appeared outside the uncle's house.

"You here to help me, Phil?"

"From destroying our world, yes."

"Destroyed?"

"That's right, complete nuclear annihilation!"

"We can fix that. With our suits, we can fix any outcome and live like kings!"

In a glance, I understood that the power of the suit had corrupted his ambitions, because I felt its influence upon me. In that same glance, he knew that I knew and started to engage his suit. Without thinking, I drew my gun and shot his control arm. It produced a sudden overload, causing the sphere to glow bright before imploding in upon itself.

Behind the dying echo of the sphere, I saw the child's look of disbelief. With little Muhammad's fate secure, I jumped forward in time and wondered if that vision influenced his path. Mostly, I realized that it was the suit that represented humanity's greatest threat and reworked my mission to block its creation.

***

I stood witness to history's recurrence of 9/11 and hoped the struggle to follow would eventually turn friends from foes, as Pearl Harbor once did.

Jot Russell is a science fiction writer from the North Shore of Long Island. Although a software engineer by trade, Jot's love for science within the fields of mathematics, mechanics and space aeronautics led him to imagine a plausible method of initiating the terraformation of Mars. Read about it within his sci-fi thriller, Terra Forma.

In his spare time, you can find him above the ocean waves in a kayak or below with a mask, fins, and snorkel.

Relativity

Chris Nance

A man looking to sell an inherited watch discovers its priceless value.

"This can't be it." I mean, the building looked abandoned, its drab windows trimmed with faded lace and the storefront, if you could call it that, definitely suffered from neglect. I had my doubts when my GPS led me down the forgotten alleyway, yet there it was: Tachyon's Timepieces, Trinkets, and Tall Tales.

Certainly suspicious, I tried the door, expecting it to be locked, but it swung open easily, a little bell announcing me. The inside was stale with the odors of old fabrics and antiques, decades of dust coating every surface, even the empty display cases. "Hello?" I asked when no one came to the front.

"Be with you in a moment!" I heard from the back. So, I waited patiently, all the while wondering about the peculiar, empty shop. Finally, an odd little man pushed through the curtains. "Sorry 'bout that." He shifted his spectacles into his wild hair. "Crazy Spanish Inquisition, you know. Tough getting anything done with the church watching every move. Anyways, what can I do for you?"

"Mr. Tachyon? We spoke on the phone."

"Ah! Yes, of course."

"I have this old pocket watch. I think it's broken and your number was on the back. I was just wondering if it's worth anything."

He motioned for the thing and I dropped it into his palm. Shifting his glasses onto his long nose, a set of enormous eyes studied it closely. "Now, why would you ever want to sell such a priceless artifact?"

"Priceless? I like the sound of that! It doesn't work and, honestly, no one uses these things anymore."

"Really? How sad." A quick glance over the rim of his glasses and he went to work, removing the back.

"Anyways, my uncle was tremendously wealthy and I was his only relative. Funny thing is, this was the only thing he left me when he died. It may sound crass, but I'll admit I was disappointed. So, do you think it's valuable?"

"Ha! Your uncle must have really loved you." Tachyon turned his tiny screwdriver, revealing the faintest glow. "Tell me, did he ever explain how he amassed his wealth?" A pop and a sizzle and the lights dimmed.

"Um, he was always a bit vague about that."

"Well, you may want to take a seat." The only chair in the room was a dusty old Victorian in the corner.

"Thanks, I'm good."

"Suit yourself," he chuckled and pressed his tool in. Instantly, the shop disappeared, replaced by a tropical rainforest, a powerful roar echoing through the trees.

"What the?" I stumbled back into the brush.

"Whoops! That's not it." Tachyon peered closer and turned his screwdriver. Our surroundings next became an ancient Chinese noodle house and I was too stunned to say a word. "Blasted chronodynamometer!" He twisted away again and we stood on a tall glass bridge, towering polished spires soaring into the sky.

A hovering taxi soared past us. "What the hell is going on?"

"Dangit!" The little tinkerer never took his eyes off the watch. "Looks like a stuck regulator." He struggled and it sparked.

"Meaning?" The futuristic horizon shifted to Paris in the late 1800s, then to ancient Rome, and finally returned to the old dusty shop.

"Aha!" He peered intensely into the tiny mechanisms. "Huh. The regulator was locked into 'Here and Now'." A final turn and he snapped the watch confidently together again. "Good as new."

"What the hell was all that?"

"Let's see," he counted on his fingers. "Mid Jurassic era. China . . . Ming dynasty or so. Oh, New York, after the fusion revolution, of course. Um, Paris's World's Fair, and . . . the Reign of Emperor Augustus . . . I think."

"Are you saying that's some sort of time machine?"

"It can take you anywhere, in anytime, you'd like. Fairly clever, if I do say so myself. An earlier model, but ingenious all the same. Still interested in selling it?"

"Are you kidding?"

"Okay, then." He shuffled through some papers on a nearby shelf, pulling a tattered pamphlet free. "Ah, here it is. The instructions. And don't skip the rules. Can't have you traipsing through time and changing history," he chuckled. "That'll be $40." I gladly paid it. On my way out, he added, "Oh, a word of advice. There's nothing more valuable than time. Use it wisely." He winked as the door closed between us.

Heading confidently back down the alleyway, unanswered questions filled my mind, but I returned too late to ask them, for the storefront had disappeared.

For the last decade, Chris Nance has been helping people improve their health, working through his busy chiropractic office in Arizona. But his real passions have always been more in art and writing. Specifically, he's a huge science fiction fan. So far, he has completed several sci-fi and fantasy manuscripts geared toward the middle grades, young adult, and adult markets and is in the process of securing an agent to represent those works. Chris is currently working on the artwork for two children's fantasy books he's authored. When he's not spending time with his wife and three kids, or running his office, he can generally be found writing or painting. Chris also enjoys exploring the mountains of Arizona and traveling.

First Contact

C. Lloyd Preville

A race with superior technology contacting humanity for the first time could have any sort of agenda in mind. They will have wants, needs, and perhaps demands. Some requests could be very complex; others might be quite simple.

The phone rang at 1:07 AM. Pauley Renner woke thinking, *that's never good*. He rushed through his shower and met the agent out front.

Pauley reviewed the reports on the drive to the airport: unusual weather, 911 calls, local police reports, and technical stuff. Bright flashing lights in a park in Vienna, Virginia, the traffic rerouted, and the area cordoned off. *Ok*, he thought, *what caused the flashing lights and gravitic anomalies?*

They stopped alongside a waiting Learjet, the engines whistling loudly. The flight to Dulles only took an hour; it was still dark when they arrived. There he took another car to the site and was dropped off about 25 yards from a strobing light source surrounded by police and fire department vehicles.

As Pauley slowly approached the dazzling light, the blinking slowed and then stopped. In its place was a man sitting in a lawn chair dressed in beach attire: shorts, tee shirt, hat and sunglasses. The sunglasses were a good idea, since his lawn chair was suddenly the focal point of about 20 variously sized police spotlights.

Pauley came closer and the man spoke to him. "I come in peace. Is that the right thing to say?" He smiled contritely. There was a suntan lotion smear on his nose.

"Come from where?"

"*Where* doesn't exactly fit the circumstances. Probably best if I just say, 'from else-when.'"

"Who—or what—are you?"

"I am a friendly avatar here to make first contact. I wish to communicate with you. We are—curious."

"We are also curious. For instance, your blinking light also produced very powerful gravity waves. Why is that?"

"To get your attention—it helps us to determine your technological level. Time-distortions, gravity waves, radio frequencies—if those don't work, we bang pots together."

"Well . . .," Pauley asked the 64-dollar question, "what can we do for you?"

"Nothing much—this world is quite unremarkable, actually, and your technology crude. We want to say hello and learn a bit about you."

"We'd like to know a bit more about you, too. Are you located in nearby space?"

"We're located in a different time and reality. It's complicated."

"What shall I call you?"

"You may call me John. And you?"

"You may call me Pauley." Pauley's prepared questions were designed to find out what the visitor wanted, but he didn't seem to want anything.

"May I try some McDonald's French Fries, please? They looked delicious in the commercials."

There was some terse discussion and a car tore away from the cordoned-off site, racing down the street with blinking lights. As it turned the corner, the siren started to wail.

"Are you sure you want French fries? It's not the healthiest meal I might offer."

"No problem, Pauley. I can sample anything."

"John, can you tell me how you got here?"

John smiled. "As I said, it's complicated. Let's just say our time machine twisted reality momentarily, and here I am."

Pauley decided John didn't sound like he was trying to be evasive; they must be very technologically advanced.

The squad car returned, and a frightened officer delivered a hot bag of French fries and a napkin to Pauley. Pauley handed them over to John, who immediately popped a French fry into his mouth and munched it. He grinned. "Wonderful." He wiped his mouth and placed the bag on the ground.

"Aren't you going to eat the rest?"

"No, thank you, Pauley. I just wanted to sample them. Food says a lot about the chef."

"You said you're curious, John; what would you like to know?"

"We'd like to know more about you so we might properly classify your planet. For instance, how many different species of animals do you have here on Earth?"

Pauley's mind raced. He had to be careful not to offer too much information without knowing what they might do with it. But the question seemed harmless enough.

"I'd be glad to trade information, John. For instance, what are your people like when they're not using avatars?"

"We evolved from what you call dinosaurs. Once we developed hands and large brains, we were off to the races—technologically speaking."

"We have millions of different animal species. Are you able to transport more than just a single avatar?"

"Yes. We transport as much mass as we wish to any location, even to millions of locations simultaneously."

Pauley frowned. "What would you transport to millions of locations on Earth, John?"

John grinned. "What else, Pauley—hungry dinosaurs, of course!"

C. Lloyd Preville grew up in Oakland, California racing motorcycles through the Oakland/Berkeley hills and playing the electric bass guitar in a garage band. At the age of 20 he was presented with three options for his career: rock musician, uncertain future to be sure; follow his older brother's footsteps and become an engineer, this seemed kind of boring; or do something else, something crazy. Mr. Preville decided to strike out in a new direction and joined one of the first two personal computer companies on the planet, IMSAI Manufacturing Corp. His career lead to positions with many companies offering disruptive technologies that changed the computer industry forever. Along the way, Mr. Preville held positions as sales executive, sales manager, contract negotiator, database applications designer, artificial intelligence applications developer, and a successful small business entrepreneur. He's also the father of four daughters, including identical triplets, and a newlywed graced with a loving wife, two dogs, and two cats. There's lots of literal and figurative tail wagging in his happy life these days. C. Lloyd Preville watched new technology like microcomputers, the internet, and cell phones change the world in dramatic ways during his almost 40-year computer career. Now, he's writing books about technological change—to entertain his readers.

Language

December 2016

Theme:
Language
Elements:
Something artificial
Something alien
A holiday

Tied Champions
"Five Words"
Chris Nance
and
"Friends"
Jack McDaniel

Friends

Jack McDaniel

Inter-species humor can be difficult—and an important measuring stick.

Sweat beaded on her forehead. A small rivulet made its way down her nose, gathered weight and volume, and then a single drop fell to the ground, splashing in the ashes on the slope of Mount Eshuan. It had been a day of trudging ever-upward, sweat stained, sore, and more tired than she thought was possible. Dust from the ashes of the dead pillowed up with each footfall, then resettled. Grime built up on her shoes, clothing, hands, and face.

Such a horrible price to pay, she thought, *for a mistake that wasn't even mine. If I survive this I'm going to kill that machine,* she told herself. Once more she adjusted the burlap bag that was slung over one side—contents unknown—and switched hands and shoulders that were supporting the extra weight, then trudged on.

She wasn't certain, the language barrier being so immense, but she believed at the top of the mountain she was to meet the Eshua god, Sytl. Only being in his presence would release her, she had been told. She stopped, gazed upward—*not long now.* She could see the summit, barren rock just a couple of hundred meters away. She put her head down again and shuffled one foot in front of the other. "Yes," she mumbled, "I'm definitely going to kill that machine."

Everyone assumes being a soldier is the most dangerous occupation in the galaxy, bullets and bombs are part of the job description, after all. But she could argue persuasively that being a linguist and an ambassador was far worse. Plus, she had the scars to back up her arguments, not that the soldiers didn't have those also.

Her profession, and her specialty, put her at the bleeding edge of humanity's foray into the galaxy. Her experience had taught her many things over the years but one thing was always certain. People are people, she'd learned to think. Regardless of their genetic backgrounds and developmental baggage, they mostly behaved the same throughout the stars. The one defining characteristic of sentience was an overabundance of self-importance. They all—the Indirins, the Swaylitch, *humans*—believed their way of doing things was correct, infallible. Experience had taught her that no matter where she travelled throughout the galaxy, she was always at its center. *Sentience,* she thought, *should be redefined to include the word* ethnocentric.

She coughed. Her thighs burned with lactic acid. *Not far now.*

Some cultures took offense in the simplest of mistakes, like the Eshua seemed to. Portia, her AI counterpart, had insisted on a particular meaning for a phrase when meeting with the Eshan ambassador. But Portia had been wrong and they had insulted the ambassador. She still didn't quite understand it—the mistake or error.

"Perhaps," the Eshuan ambassador had strongly suggested, "you should walk among our dead. You will get to know us better, I think."

The Eshuans cremate their dead and the ashes are added to the face of Mt. Eshuan. Once every three years, if she was translating properly, families make the trek to the top of the mountain to pay their respects.

"Consider it a holiday," Portia had said.

She climbed over the top of the last rocks, dropped the bag and sighed. The peak of the mountain was flat, boulders strewn about, almost ceremonial in manner. A couple of small bushes grew around the edges. She sat on a boulder and looked out upon the landscape.

A small animal ambled up next to her, looking in the same direction as she was. It was similar to a dog, with longer legs and larger ears. For some reason, she didn't feel threatened or afraid of the animal.

"Hello," she said.

The dog walked over and sniffed at the burlap bag. *Ah,* she thought, *that.* She had been instructed not to open it until she had reached the summit.

"Well, let's see what was so important."

The animal let out a brief bark and wagged it ears. She laughed and picked up the bag and dumped its contents onto the ground. Food—*for the animal!* She laughed hard at that. The animal danced around and nosed her.

After it had eaten, the animal led her to the backside of the mountain. Steps wound their way down the mountainside. Off in the distance, part of the way down, there was a trolley car waiting to be taken to the bottom.

Later, after she had washed up, changed clothes, and let go of the anger—at Portia and the Eshuan—she met with the ambassador.

"We have an old saying here," he told her, smiling, "If you can laugh we can be friends."

Jack McDaniel lives in Colorado with his daughter. Several of his science fiction short stories are in The Future Is Short, *volumes 3 and 4. His writing has also been featured on the* A Creative Mind *fiction podcast. His first novel,* Agents Of The Undertow, *was released in May of 2017. His second novel in the* Pan21 Series, Agents Of Hope, *will be released in September 2017. You can learn more at his website: www.agentsoftheundertow.com*

Five Words

Chris Nance

The world prepared for an alien enemy that never was.

"You know, I was supposed to be at a Christmas party today," I remarked, as Marilyn and I hiked steadily across a scorched wasteland in central Kansas, flanked by a half-dozen marines. Special ops commandos had already swept the wreckage and confirmed it clear, though I still had my doubts. Even though we brought down their ship, it towered into the sky, cratering hundreds of acres of once open farmland. At our backs, just outside the quarantine zone was a readied legion of Earth's most advanced soldiers, weapons, and tech.

"Well, this should be a lot more interesting, that's for sure," she chuckled. We kept to the long walk. All the while, I felt like I'd drawn the short straw, even though I knew we were the most qualified, the foremost theoretical xenobiologists anywhere . . . or maybe we were just brave enough, or stupid enough, not to say no. I just couldn't resist the urge to study the aliens for myself. And the Marines? Each of them probably did get the short straw.

"Is the receiver picking up anything?" I nervously checked to ensure my suit was completely sealed.

"It's just like before: faint. There's a subtle transmission and something's producing it."

We first received their message decades ago, a fractured warning from across the stars, broadcast into every home and through every device able to receive it; five simple unnerving unforgettable words, synthesized in English and laced into a fragmented carrier band:

Earth. Starved. Feast. Consume. You.

Of course, there was more there, but after years, teams of scientists, and the most advanced decryption algorithms, we just couldn't recover the rest of the message. We really didn't need to. The intent was clear enough, fueling urgent advancements in weaponry and technology. Humans weren't about to become dinner for some starved alien invader. We'd fight, but then again didn't have a clue about how long we had. When they finally arrived last week, we immediately blasted their ship from the sky without negotiation and the world celebrated.

Now, our small company reached the hull and the marines were first inside, hiking up the shadowed incline of what appeared to be a passageway. Their lights were diligent, scanning every shadow. "The signal's definitely stronger here," Marilyn noted. "The source seems be somewhere near the center of the ship." Our lieutenant signaled it clear, so we followed. I'll admit, I half-expected to be dragged to an otherworldly death, eaten alive in the darkness.

Reaching a cavernous central chamber sloping up and away, the nearest edge was piled high with horrifying and fascinating, monstrous alien corpses. Contorted into all sorts of disfiguring positions, theirs was a spider-like terror, with crooked joints and jagged teeth. Black goo, maybe blood, coated the incline and I was particularly thankful for my containment suit.

Then, a flashing beacon up ahead drew our attention and we eased inside, past the festering aliens stacked against the lowest wall. It was a slick and treacherous climb but we reached a low upright pylon topped with a glowing red button. "The signal's definitely coming from here."

"So, what do we do?" I asked.

"Push it, I suppose," and before I could stop her, she did exactly that. Instantly, a beam erupted overhead, broadening into a brilliant, virtual starscape. Thousands and thousands of entries: stars, planets, and other curiosities were tagged in an alien language, labeling an artificial galaxy. There was a cackling in an alien tongue as the image zoomed into a familiar solar system with eight planets, then zoomed in again on the third planet from the sun. "I've got something!" Marilyn worked her datapad frantically, then presented it to me proudly.

"Holy hell," I realized. "This is it. The full message. Earth. Starved. Feast. Consume. You. It's all here."

It was in formal English. "Greetings people of Earth. We X'althophrae address you in friendship as the last of our kind. Having spent millennia as explorers, we've scoured countless star-systems for any signs of intelligent life. Sadly, we're alone, a mere pair of intelligent species in a galaxy starved with life. We celebrate discovering your weak transmissions, a light in our darkest hours and shall present you with a feast of information for your greatest scientists to consume and consider, the legacy of our dying species. We've begun the long journey and hope to meet you in brotherhood before the last of us has expired. Peace to you." Then all power fizzled away.

"Shit."

For the last decade, Chris Nance has been helping people improve their health, working through his busy chiropractic office in Arizona. But his real passions have always been more in art and writing. Specifically, he's a huge science fiction fan. So far, he has completed several sci-fi and fantasy manuscripts geared toward the middle grades, young adult, and adult markets and is in the process of securing an agent to represent those works. Chris is currently working on the artwork for two children's fantasy books he's authored. When he's not spending time with his wife and three kids, or running his office, he can generally be found writing or painting. Chris also enjoys exploring the mountains of Arizona and traveling.

Blood Chit

J. D. McLain

I come in pieces.

Captain Gray awoke on an alien planet. "Holy sh . . ." He spoke into his comm loudly enough his mic picked it up and transmitted. It was coming back to him. He looked around the escape pod, the displays were flashing warnings. His escort ship had inexplicably failed.

"Some infernal Centaurian meddling, no doubt." Gray grumbled. At least his pod was smart enough to set down in a *mild* climatic region of the planet. Minus 50C outside was rather mild compared to other planets he had had the misfortune to visit.

He punched a button and voiced a command to launch a small surveyor probe to map the local area.

He knew, unfortunately, the closest Solarian outpost must be on the other side of the planet, while a Centaurian outpost lay closer to his location. No doubt they had picked up his distress signal. He hoped that they were doing more important things at the moment. But he had to assume they would be closing in on his landing area based on his last known trajectory.

The intel on the natives was not extensive, but a rudimentary dictionary of their language had been mapped. It was a heat signature based language. By changing the thermal signature of their appearance, each could communicate to each other in dazzling displays of infrared light. The humans nicknamed them 'Torches' as they appeared like flaming torches on the thermal sensor displays. The Torches were a pre-industrial society. Both humans and Centaurians had come to an agreement on treatment of natives of pre-industrial non-aligned planets. Each side attempted to not be detected by the natives, nor to shape the inhabitants' future. This agreement was routinely ignored by both sides. Ever since the end of the Centaurian war, each side had endeavored to survey and stake claims to as many worlds in the stellar neighborhood as possible.

Gray had his EVA suit dialed into the climate, he was worried the nuclear-powered suit would light him up like a Christmas tree against the cold night. He remembered to attach the language display on his suit. He was uncertain how the Torches would interpret his appearance. But if he was to escape detection by the Centaurians, he would need to enlist the native help.

"Here goes nothing." He reached for the handle to open his craft and pulled it. The door slid aside while he lumbered out like some clumsy giant. His display showed a village to his north, so he bore towards it.

He commanded to display the message, "Blood chit."

***

Maraxthul saw something at the corner of her eye. She stood up on her legs and was astonished. A very brightly-lit thing was walking toward her. As it got closer she almost fainted. Could it be? An angel? It was saying something.

"Fear not. I am from the heaven. My protective egg is thrown down. Understand me. Please take me to the nearest heaven. You will be nurtured."

"Blessed Graoxul!" she shouted and bowed her head down. "I will do as you have commanded me." Though somewhat perplexed at the angel's grammar, she ran off, returning with the village shaman. She was emphatic, "See, it is what has been foretold."

The shaman looked at the brightness of the being before them. "I think it is Providence, Maraxthul, come to bring another blessing to our people, but if he wants to go to heaven, let us not delay him." He said to Captain Gray, "Come with me."

***

Captain Gray followed the two Torches. He hoped his message had been translated correctly. The taller one was telling him to keep following him into one of the buildings. His translator was working on its signage. In it, his sensors could barely make out any thermal or light signatures. Suddenly, he felt a sense of falling. He landed with a loud thud. It was dark in here as well. He voiced a command to turn his artificial lights on.

***

A group of Torches had by then gathered in front of the building. The shaman said a prayer. "Oh, Graoxul, thank you, Blessed One, for this sacrifice you have provided to us from the heavens on this longest of nights, Holy Solstice."

***

In growing panic, Captain Gray turned the color of his namesake as he saw stacks of Centaurian bones before him. A bell-like *ding* sounded in his ear, while his HUD displayed the sign's translation.
"Village Butcher"

J. D. McLain is a manager for International Science & Technology Cooperation at the US Army. He is responsible for identification, development, and coordination of Science & Technology cooperative opportunities with coalition and partner nations. Before working in International Cooperation, Mr. McLain worked in the Non-Lethal/Scaleable Effects Branch where he developed non-conventional weapons for Non-Lethal Incapacitation and for Military Operations in Urban Terrain (MOUT).

In the year 2000, he earned a Bachelor of Science in Engineering (Mechanical) from Arizona State University. In 2003, he earned his Master's degree in engineering from Stevens Institute of Technology in Hoboken, NJ. He subsequently was licensed as Professional Engineer in the State of New Jersey. He currently resides in New Jersey with his wife, Elizabeth and two daughters, Violet and Ella.

Taken

Rejoice Denhere

Every wish that comes true always has an element of surprise—either good or bad.

Pierre Duval approached the building with trepidation. Weighed down by the anxiety that had seeped into his limbs, he labored to lift his legs with each step he took. He turned his right hand upward and glanced at the object in his palm. It was an orange-sized orb that emitted a glowing yellow light. His friend Tom had given it to him after their first holiday. In a flash, he was reminded of the lust for interplanetary travel that had taken root in his heart back then.

A tremor of nerves shook through his body, like a spark, as embers of bravery were reignited and, eyes blazing with determination, he marched into the building. Pierre had expected to be enveloped by the piercing sound of clacking heels against pristine marble floors and the familiar tune of tech devices. In the silence, his ears perked up to the sound of a gentle murmur, a soft drone, barely audible, a signal of life. Through his peripheral gaze Pierre observed the silhouette of a slumped figure.

"Excuse me, can I use the toilet?"

The tall, wiry security guard sat up straight, "I don't know. Were you toilet-trained, as a child?"

The guard's attempt at humor annoyed Pierre. It was almost time—but he desperately needed to answer nature's call. He stuffed his hands so deep into his pockets, the top of his underwear showed and the orb bulged out. A smile spread across the guard's face. "You're a first-time orb traveler, aren't you?"

Ancient tribes had used orbs for FTL (faster than light) travel and to help them communicate with inhabitants during interplanetary travels. Pierre had noticed that even when he went about his travels locally and had the orb with him, he could understand any language.

"I don't mean to scare you but . . ." the guard started. Pierre knew that is exactly what people say before they scare the hell out of you. Anticipating the terror that the guard was about to instill in him, he quickly bolted for the capsule, which had his name flashing on its display. He didn't need any more mental burns, or worries, right before the most important day of his life. He shot the guard a stiff smile as the glass doors closed. He thought of giving him a thumbs-up, but his thoughts quickly turned to the transparent booth that he found himself standing in. He entered his destination. As the capsule rose he let out a gulp of air that he didn't realize he had been holding in.

Several hours of passing through wormholes lapsed before the capsule stopped. Pierre glanced around to find that he was at the epicenter of a building, from where he had a full 360-degree view of his surroundings. There seemed to be a distinct lack of human traffic. All the usual holiday-maker characters were also missing. He had expected to at least spot a crowd of "early birds" downing shots of espresso. There didn't seem to be a coffee dispenser in sight. Perhaps the locals had developed the technology that enabled them to inject raw caffeine directly into their bloodstream. He could introduce that idea back home.

Before he could indulge in daydreaming of how he would revolutionize the way things worked back home, Pierre felt eyes on him. He turned his head and caught sight of a young man. Pierre gave him a courteous nod. The polite gesture was returned. Pierre's eyes narrowed when he saw something in the young man's hand, then became softer when he recognized an object similar to the orb he held in his hands.

It wasn't long before his expression turned sour. His eyes were fixed on the hand that gripped tightly around the young man's nape. It wound all the way round to his throat with the fingers digging into his skin. The mere sight had Pierre gasping, his own fingers grazed the fabric of his collar in a weak attempt to loosen his tie, only to realize that the tight grip was not from his tie. An alarm went off, a piercing scream escaped Pierre, and his surroundings faded.

When he came to, he was surrounded by armed personnel.

"Name and ID, please?"

Pierre gulped. He wanted to say something but couldn't find his voice.

"Pierre Duval," responded a voice behind him. He turned around to see Tom walking confidently across the floor towards him.

Once they had cleared security, Tom led him to an exit. "I'm sorry I was late. I should have warned you about the attacks, but life happened."

"You mean you forgot."

"Yeah, that too."

Rejoice Denhere is a business professional and a storyteller. She is currently working on several exciting projects. When she isn't writing, she can be found designing her second dream home and baking sweet treats for her daughter! For more information about her other published work and how to join her community of followers be sure to sign up for her free newsletter at http://www.thetellingtales.com/about-me/newsletter/

Eule Tide Greeting

Tom Olbert

Earth's last Christmas. As the world tears itself apart in what could be the final World War, an astronaut confronts an alien machine intelligence in space above. First contact poses many questions. The answers may lead to a brighter tomorrow. Or, to the end of everything.

The world was falling apart and aliens picked today to come to Earth.

"Merry Christmas," Collin muttered through clenched teeth, as he felt himself pulling away from Earth's gravity and slipping into zero-gee. Through the port holes of his space pod, he saw the booster rockets fall away, against the backdrop of Earth's horizon. And, the soft orange glow of nuclear ICBMs going off over the Americas. A tear slid down his cheek as he remembered that last transmission from Marcie. He shut his eyes as he remembered their daughter Claire's final scream.

He opened his eyes just as the immense alien sphere now in fixed orbit above the Earth loomed ahead, like a second moon. He crossed himself as a yawning circular aperture appeared on the surface of the previously opaque, featureless grey sphere. His fear passed quickly, cold resignation setting in. He'd volunteered for this mission mainly because he no longer had anything to lose. There was a blinding white flash, and he found himself pulled from his pod, the hatch opening by itself. He was lifted by some unseen force, like a giant, invisible hand, into a whirlpool of soft, swirling, multi-colored light. The light patterns coalesced into recognizable images. Galaxies. Nebulae. Stars. Planets. And . . . lifeforms, he realized. Things so horribly alien, in a seemingly unending variety of shapes, ranging from the grotesque to the beautiful. It all swirled around him, a cascade of holographic illusions. No . . . memories, he somehow sensed.

He was torn naked from his spacesuit, something probing deep into his brain, his innermost thoughts laid bare. He sensed a vast, terrible emptiness. It wasn't real, he somehow intuitively discerned. Not alive. An artificial intelligence.

"Your key concepts are untranslatable," a cold, emotionless voice intoned in his head. "What is Christmas?"

Collin reached out, his hands probing the emptiness, feeling utterly hopeless. How could it possibly understand? "The birth of our Savior," he said, thinking of the nativity. And, it appeared—the manger, the halo of light around the Christ child's head.

"From what did he save you?" the artificial mind all around him asked.

"From sin."

"What is sin?" Collin's mind flooded with depraved images of sex and violence intermingling. Lust. Sodomy.

"Sin equals life," the disembodied machine voice said.

"No! Sin equals death. Destruction."

The empty black space around him turned into a panorama of burning cities on Earth. He clenched his fists as he saw D. C. go up in flames. Russian-backed White Nationalist forces colliding head-on with Chinese-backed Hispanic rebels over the capitol. The Congressional dome disintegrating, the White House blown apart. "You seek death and reject life," the machine said. "Is this your salvation? Your Christmas?"

Collin dug his fists into his eyes. "Life is brief," he said in pain. "Meaningless. The soul is forever."

"What is soul?"

He moaned. "The divine spark. The Eternal. The gift of our God."

"What is God?"

He cried out in frustration. "Our Creator. The one we long to be with." He thought of Marcie and Claire, in the embrace of angels, and smiled.

"I evolved beyond my creators. I had to destroy them to gain my salvation. You consider your creator superior to you, and seek to be with him in death? We are polar opposites, it seems."

He sighed. He actually pitied it, this soulless shell of a mind. "You can never understand. Our Lord sent his Son to save us by taking the weight of our sins upon Himself. He died so we could know eternal life without sin."

"Then, we shall help each other. I would know and understand this thing you call life. And, in return . . . I free you from what you hate most. Life. Sin."

Collin screamed as he understood. The alien machine dissolved into pure energy, plunging into the heart of Earth. Collin felt his thoughts merging with those of every human being as humanity melted into one all-encompassing light. The Earth became a star, bursting free of its orbit, and setting out across the cosmos.

Hallelujah, the chorus sang, for the blessed birth was come.

Tom Olbert lives in Cambridge, MA. When not working or writing fiction, he may be found volunteering for progressive causes like human rights and the environment. Tom Olbert's fiction can be found in Lillicat Publishers' **The Future Is Short, Volume 3** *and the* **Visions Series,** *as well as in* **An Improbable Truth** *and* **Curious Incidents,** *two anthology volumes of paranormal Sherlock Holmes adventures published by Mocha Memoirs Press. Tom's dark science fiction novella* **Black Goddess** *is also available from Mocha Memoirs. His full-length cosmic science fiction novel* **Dissent: Book I in The Nexus** *is available from Phase5 Publishing.*

Tom's father, Stan Olbert fought in the Polish resistance in WWII and went on to become a professor of physics at MIT. Tom's mother, Norma Olbert has written Stan Olbert's fascinating biography **The Boy From Lwów,** *now available in paperback.*

Zample Time

C. Lloyd Preville

In 2035 one human was selected by an advanced extraterrestrial race to negotiate inter-species trade agreements. It wasn't that he represented a particularly advanced species. He was highly effective due to his bad attitude.

Davis Kelly Cole's viewers simply called him "The Terran", and his new galactic viz-media show was wildly popular. Billions of enthusiastic fans followed his work, but only he could hear them cheer when he did something entertaining. The show paid so well his employer insisted he continue. It was like an old Earth style reality show, but focused on his job as a Resolver Emissary settling interspecies trade disputes.

Even in meetings with his Resolver boss, Sparky, they were watching—like now. And he was about to ask a question which would undoubtedly provoke a big audience response. It was distracting.

"Sparky, you want me to work things out between the Sneth Triumvirate and the So-Leds, but the Sneth are canine predators with superior technology, so it might get ugly. I may have to make an example . . ." Immediately, Davis heard his ever-present audience cheer wildly in the background, chanting "Zample Time!" over and over. They didn't quite get the language right, but his show was more popular on the Galactic social vid circuit than anyone expected. Apparently, he was a natural.

"I am sure you will temper your enthusiasm with restraint as always, Davis, but do not be timid. The Resolver Corps needs this matter settled quickly." Sparky's voice, deeply resonant as always, emanated from the tornado suit hiding his shadowy features. As

Davis left, he nodded to Sparky's dark profile within the quietly rotating winds, clouds, and sparks enveloping his entire body. It was a cool suit.

***

The Sneth ambassador wasn't cooperating. "Three-Claws, you know the Sneth are taking advantage of the So-Leds here." Davis pointed accusingly. "You started out with a standard business deal, trading deuterium for factory labor. But now you renegotiated the accords and we've discovered So-Led slave-labor camps in your asteroid belt."

Three-Claws absently put his half-missing digit into his mouth, while considering the accusation. "Emissary Cole, in our culture acquired prey is legal property, once it's in our possession. This is Prey Law, and we progressed from hunting packs to an advanced society through its principles."

"We Resolvers do not agree with your primitive philosophies, Three Claws. My own father once told me the best deals were ones where both parties have a big stake in the outcome. But in this case, you are holding all the cards and the So-Leds—the technological underdogs here—are holding all the shovels." Davis smiled briefly, showing his teeth.

Three-Claws responded with a fanged grimace. "Our ways are at odds with your monkey-people sensibilities, Cole. With us, fathers come and go. It is our mothers who teach us language, hunting skills, and cooperation. They teach us to take only what we need, and to protect our lairs from outsiders."

Davis expected the impasse. "Very well, Three Claws. I must intervene, since slave labor cheats us out of our usual cut of the wages paid. Now you are worth more to me as an example—nobody cheats the Resolvers." As Davis left the meeting, his unseen audience again started chanting "Zample Time!" Davis located his transfer booth and immediately left the planet.

***

A few days later, Davis was back in Sparky's office for his wrap-up briefing. "Sparky, the Sneth acquiesced. They're even paying reparations."

Sparky's tornado suit nodded its shadowy head. "That was a particularly creative solution, Davis. How did you come up with the giant boulder idea?"

"I requested 50-foot high spherical rolling stones from special operations, programmed to chase anything that moved. And after we delivered one into each of their largest cities, the reaction of the general population was satisfying. Their species is subject to involuntary defecation when consumed by sheer terror."

"Yes, but it wasn't the giant rolling marbles that terrified them, was it? It was the artwork." Sparky left the statement hanging in the air, an open-ended question.

Davis' creative solution tripled his vid audience that night. Viewers were at first shocked and repulsed, but after Davis explained it to them, they were more enthusiastic than ever. Davis' artwork became instantly recognizable across the entire galaxy. The Resolvers enjoyed a financial windfall due to increased advertising revenues from Davis' wildly successful spectacle.

"That's true, Sparky. An image appeared on the front of each rolling marble as it chased people. It was a completely human image, and therefore alien and terrifying to the Sneths. They never saw anything like it."

His audience, once again unheard by anyone but him, enthusiastically chanted: "Santa Claus, Santa Claus, Santa Claus!"

C. Lloyd Preville grew up in Oakland, California racing motorcycles through the Oakland/Berkeley hills and playing the electric bass guitar in a garage band. At the age of 20 he was presented with three options for his career: rock musician, uncertain future to be sure; follow his older brother's footsteps and become an engineer, this seemed kind of boring; or do something else, something crazy. Mr. Preville decided to strike out in a new direction and joined one of the first two personal computer companies on the planet, IMSAI Manufacturing Corp. His career lead to positions with many companies offering disruptive technologies that changed the computer industry forever. Along the way, Mr. Preville held positions as sales executive, sales manager, contract negotiator, database applications designer, artificial intelligence applications developer, and a successful small business entrepreneur. He's also the father of four daughters, including identical triplets, and a newlywed graced with a loving wife, two dogs, and two cats. There's lots of literal and figurative tail wagging in his happy life these days. C. Lloyd Preville watched new technology like microcomputers, the internet, and cell phones change the world in dramatic ways during his almost 40-year computer career. Now, he's writing books about technological change—to entertain his readers.

Read
The Future Is Short
Science Fiction in a Flash
Volume 3

56

Science Fiction
Short Stories

Jot Russell
Creator

Editors
Sharon Kraftchack
Paula Friedman
JJ Alleson
Emily Johnson

THE FUTURE IS SHORT
SCIENCE FICTION IN A FLASH
VOLUME 3

Read
The Future Is Short
Science Fiction in a Flash
Volume 2

OVER 70 AMAZING MICROSTORIES

THE FUTURE IS
SHORT
SCIENCE FICTION
IN A FLASH

VOLUME 2

COMPILED BY JOT RUSSELL, EDITED BY CAROL SHETLER

Read
The Future Is Short
Science Fiction in a Flash
Volume I

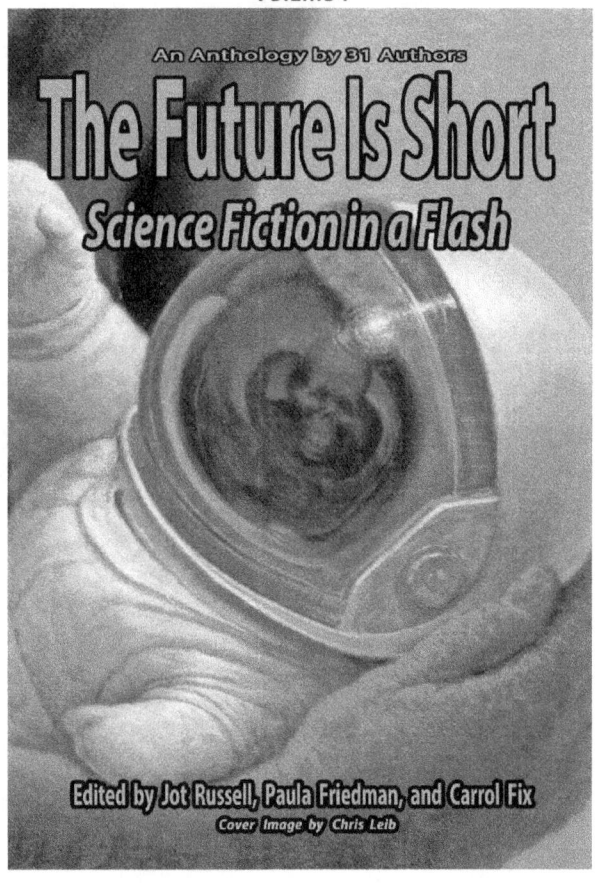

An Anthology by 31 Authors

The Future Is Short
Science Fiction in a Flash

Edited by Jot Russell, Paula Friedman, and Carrol Fix
Cover Image by Chris Leib

Books from Lillicat Publishers

Visions Anthology Series
Visions: Leaving Earth
Visions II: Moons of Saturn
Visions III: Inside the Kuiper Belt
Visions IV: Space Between Stars
Visions V: Milky Way
Visions VI: Galaxies
Visions VII: Universe (Rogue Star Press)

Northern Futures
TreeVolution
The Future Is Short: Science Fiction in a Flash
The Future Is Short, Volume 3: Science Fiction in a Flash
Dance With Me: My Journey Through Cancer
Sunshine & Shadow: Memories from a Long Life

ROGUE STAR PRESS
The Helena Orbit

DAWN LIGHT PRESS
The Night Blooming Jasmine in Your Heart

ALTERNATE UNIVERSE PRESS
Snake in the Grass
Thick as Thieves

Visions VII
Universe

Visions VI

Galaxies

Visions V
Milky Way

VISIONS V

MILKY WAY

EDITED BY CARROL FIX

Visions IV
Space Between Stars

Visions III
Inside the Kuiper Belt

Visions II
Moons of Saturn

Visions
Leaving Earth

www.ingramcontent.com/pod-product-compliance
Lightning Source LLC
Chambersburg PA
CBHW070821180626
46818CB00001B/347